HOT STUFF!

The Hardys peered into several of the dressing rooms. Most of them were empty, but Joe discovered a gorgeous young woman in one of them. She was dressed in  fiery red hair was lo

"I definitely thi Joe whispered as h om.

The woman whirled around in surprise, holding a long-necked green bottle to her lips with one hand and clutching a lit torch with the other.

"Sorry to interrupt," Frank said.

The woman whipped the bottle away from her lips and swung the torch up at the same time, spewing out whatever was in her mouth.

The liquid hit the torch flame and shot a hot blast of fire across the room—right at Frank!

Books in THE HARDY BOYS CASEFILES™ Series

Available from ARCHWAY Paperbacks

THE HARDY BOYS CASEFILES NO. 98

MURDER BY MAGIC

FRANKLIN W. DIXON

AN ARCHWAY PAPERBACK
Published by POCKET BOOKS
New York   London   Toronto   Sydney   Tokyo   Singapore

This book is a work of fiction. Names, characters, places and incidents are products of the author's imagination or are used fictitiously. Any resemblance to actual events or locales or persons, living or dead, is entirely coincidental.

AN ARCHWAY PAPERBACK *Original*

An Archway Paperback published by
POCKET BOOKS, a division of Simon & Schuster Inc.
1230 Avenue of the Americas, New York, NY 10020

ISBN: 0-671-88209-0

First Archway Paperback printing April 1995

10 9 8 7 6 5 4 3 2 1

Cover art by Brian Kotzky

Printed in the U.S.A.

IL 6+

Chapter

1

"WHAT'S SHE DOING NOW?" Frank Hardy whispered, moving up in the shadows to stand next to his brother.

"Shh!" Joe hissed, his sharp blue eyes tracking every move the woman made. "I've almost got it figured out. I think I know how she does this one."

"Good," Frank said. "As soon as you uncover the secret, we can turn her over to the police."

Joe caught his brother's grin out of the corner of his eye. "Very funny," he muttered.

"Sorry," Frank said. "But you're acting so serious. We're not tracking international spies, you know. We're just a couple of volunteer stagehands at a magic show, watching a magician at work."

"Shh!" Joe said again, his gaze riveted on the beautiful young woman on the stage.

"What's so great about the trick she's doing?" Frank asked.

"It's not a *trick*," Joe responded, emphasizing the last word. "It's an *illusion*."

Frank shook his head. He was still getting used to Joe's new enthusiasm for the art of magic. He did find his attention being drawn back to the magician, Selina St. Dragon. She opened a large steel cage to release a huge, shaggy grizzly bear. The bear shambled out on all fours and then rose to its full eight-foot height with a growl that echoed through the theater. Selina guided the bear in a circle using only a short silver baton.

"Look at the size of him," Frank marveled.

"Just be glad you didn't have to move him onstage." The deep, warm voice came from behind Frank.

Frank turned to see the owner of the theater, a distinguished-looking man in a tuxedo, his gray hair and beard neatly trimmed. Harold Meaney, better known as Hocus-Pocus Harry, still had a boyish enthusiasm for magic, even though Frank figured him to be over seventy. The retired master magician owned and operated the Sleight of Hand, the theater, hotel, and museum of magic that were his pride and joy.

"The bear's name is Goliath," Harry said. "Selina can make him do just about anything, and no one else can control him. Last year in St. Louis he put a careless stagehand in the hospital."

Selina led the bear to the center of the stage, where he dropped down onto his front paws with a force that shook the floor.

"Stay," Selina commanded, and then she draped a shimmering gold cloth over him. Goliath roared once from beneath the cover.

"Don't be a baby," she scolded, which made Frank and most of the audience chuckle. She stood back, holding one corner of the gold cloth. Then she began to count, "One . . . two . . . three!"

With a flourish she yanked the cloth away. In Goliath's place was a pile of stuffed teddy bears. The theater shook with applause, which Selina accepted while tossing the stuffed bears into the audience.

"That was incredible!" Joe raved.

"That was *magic*," Harry said. He squeezed between the Hardys and stepped onto the stage. He went to the microphone and gestured at Selina as she threw out the last of the teddy bears. "Ladies and gentlemen, Selina St. Dragon!"

Selina continued to bow and wave until the

curtain fell and hid her from view. The spot-lights focused on Harry.

"And now," he said, "there will be a brief intermission. Stretch your legs and wet your whistles, but don't go far. You won't want to miss even a second of what's to come."

The houselights came up, and Harry returned to the wings. Harry winked at Joe, but Frank knew how worried the showman was.

"I sure hope this year's magic festival makes money for Harry," Frank said.

"Of course it will," Joe told him. "We've been coming to Harry's Sleight of Hand magic festival every year since we were little. I think Legerdemania just gets better every year."

"I agree, but I think Harry's really worried. It takes a lot of money to keep this place running, and if this year's festival isn't a huge financial success, Harry might have to close down Sleight of Hand."

"But it was a sellout tonight," Joe countered.

"Tonight's only the first night," Frank said. "There are still four more to go."

"The best magicians in the world come to Legerdemania," Joe pointed out. "The theater will be jammed every night. You'll see."

"I hope so, for Harry's sake. He's been such a good friend to us. Remember when he performed at my tenth birthday party—for free?

I just wish there was something more we could do to make the festival a success."

"Let me know if you think of anything," Joe said as he checked his short blond hair in the mirror set just offstage. "In the meantime, do you want to go out front and see Vanessa and Callie?"

"Whenever you're through admiring yourself," Frank said, but Joe caught him giving his own brown hair a quick combing with his fingers.

On the main floor of the theater, people were marching up the aisles to the lobby or standing in small groups. The buzz of many conversations filled the century-old theater.

"Hey, there are Mom, Dad, and Aunt Gertrude," Joe said, waving from the front of the auditorium. His parents waved back cheerfully. Aunt Gertrude appeared less than thrilled to see him.

"Looks like Aunt Gertrude hasn't completely forgiven you for your little milk trick this morning," Frank noted.

Joe made a face at his brother before pointing out Callie and Vanessa a dozen rows back. He led Frank in their direction.

"Are you having a good time?" Frank asked as he reached Callie Shaw, his girlfriend. Her blond hair swept across her shoulders as she turned her head and smiled at him.

"We're having a great time," Callie said. "The magicians are terrific."

Joe frowned at his girlfriend, Vanessa Bender. "What's that beside your ear?" he asked, moving closer for a better look.

"What?" Vanessa self-consciously raised her hand to her head. She was tall and slim, with deep blue-gray eyes that were now wide with surprise.

Joe reached under her long, ash blond hair, and when he pulled his hand back, he held a red rose.

"Thanks," she said, "but if you pull anything else out of my ear, I'm going to hit you with it."

"It could be worse," Frank told her. "This morning he tried to make a pitcher of milk disappear and instead drenched poor Aunt Gertrude."

"That could have happened to anyone," Joe grumbled.

"Speaking of making food disappear," Frank said, "here comes Chet."

The others turned to see their heavyset friend, Chet Morton, lumbering down the aisle with a bucket of popcorn, a soda, and a pair of hot dogs. He waved the hot dogs in greeting, but stopped a few rows back to talk to another friend. Muscular Biff Hooper was squeezed into a theater seat next to his family.

6

"Hey," Frank said, "I didn't know Biff was coming tonight."

At that moment the lights flickered, signaling the end of the intermission.

"We should be getting back to our backstage post," Joe said, tugging at his brother's arm. "I don't want to miss anything."

Frank smiled goodbye to Callie and allowed himself to be dragged away. When Joe took an interest in something, Frank knew better than to try to stand in the way.

The Hardys were back in the wings as Hocus-Pocus Harry was announcing the next act.

"Selina St. Dragon brought you the most dangerous animals from the world's remotest places," Harry said. "Now we journey to a place even more savage and mysterious—the human mind. Please join me in welcoming—Dr. Savant!"

Harry yielded the stage to a suave-looking man in a black turtleneck, black slacks, and black shoes. He could be a TV star, Joe thought, with his perfectly styled short brown hair, dark eyes that glinted in the spotlights, and mysterious smile, which had already captivated the audience.

"Good evening," Savant said in a rich and cultured voice. "It's my pleasure to be here with you tonight. Before we get started, I'll need a few volunteers to join me onstage."

Dozens of arms shot into the air as eager audience members volunteered. Joe nudged Frank's arm and nodded to the spot where Biff Hooper and his family were forcing Biff's father's arm up.

"How can I turn down such enthusiasm?" Savant declared in an amused tone as he gestured to Mr. Hooper, who was struggling not to be noticed. "You look like a man of strong intellect. Please, join me."

Biff's father blushed all the way to his receding hairline, but he gave in good-naturedly and made his way to the stage, along with five other volunteers, all handpicked by Dr. Savant.

"This should be good," Joe said in a low voice.

"It had better be," Frank replied, grinning, "or Biff's going to be in for it."

Dr. Savant began with Rosalie, a giggling, frizzy-haired blond girl in a Bayport University sweatshirt. Dr. Savant spoke softly to her and held his dark eyes inches from hers. In only a few seconds her eyes became unfocused and she stared into the far distance.

"Rosalie," Dr. Savant commanded, "you love to imitate Elvis Presley. Whenever you hear the word *parsnip,* you will feel free to indulge yourself. When I snap my fingers, you will stop, and you will not remember imitating Elvis."

He snapped his fingers directly in front of

8

her face, and she suddenly looked around, disoriented, and began to giggle.

"Shall we try it out?" he asked the audience.

Encouraged by resounding applause, he held out the microphone to the next person in line, an older woman who blinked uneasily behind thick glasses. She glanced at Rosalie and said, "Parsnip?"

Rosalie's upper lip pulled up into a sneer as she launched into "Heartbreak Hotel," strumming an imaginary guitar at the end of each line. Dr. Savant held the microphone toward her for the audience's benefit.

"You know," Joe observed, "she's not bad."

Just then, one of their fellow volunteer stagehands, a tall redheaded guy with a crew cut, jogged up behind them. "Hey, guys, they've finally got something for us to do."

Frank and Joe hated to pull themselves away before they learned Savant's plans for Biff's father, but they followed the other stagehand farther backstage to a large glass water tank. The tank was big—big enough to hold a sleek, deadly, six-foot shark that circled restlessly above a treasure chest half-buried in the sand at the bottom of the tank. A life-size grinning skeleton in pirate garb rested against the side of the treasure chest.

Frank and Joe joined a half dozen other stagehands, all athletic teenagers like themselves. At eighteen, Frank was an inch over six feet and in good shape. Joe, a year younger and an inch shorter than his brother, was even more muscular. Despite all that muscle power, moving the tank was still difficult. A slender woman in a tuxedo and a bearded man dressed as a medieval wizard in a long blue robe and pointed hat stopped to watch.

"Who in the world brought that thing?" Frank overheard the wizard ask.

"Gideon," the woman answered. "Who else? Can you imagine what it must have cost to haul that all the way from Las Vegas?"

"You hear that?" Frank asked his brother. "Isn't Gideon the one you've been dying to see?"

Joe grunted in the affirmative. "Gideon is the best magician in the world. You'll be amazed."

With a great deal of effort, they got the tank into position behind the curtain. Then Joe rushed to the wings to catch the end of Dr. Savant's act.

When Frank joined him, Savant had already hypnotized Mr. Hooper. Biff's dad was now balanced, rigid as a board, on the tips of two gleaming swords.

"Ouch," Frank murmured in awe. He noted that the audience's applause was reserved, hesitant. Nobody wanted to startle the man out of the trance while he was poised over the deadly sword blades.

Savant then replaced the swords with a pair

of straight-back chairs and helped Mr. Hooper
to his feet. Mr. Hooper came out of his trance,
and Savant encouraged the audience to applaud his participation.

"Look at him blush," Joe said, laughing.

Frank felt sorry for Biff's dad but couldn't
help chuckling. As Mr. Hooper left the stage,
stagehands removed Savant's props and the
hypnotist stepped to the microphone.

"Thank you. You're very kind. I now have
the pleasure of introducing our next act. Please
welcome the sorcerer supreme, the most
astounding master of illusion ever to take the
stage—and also my little brother—Gideon the
Great!"

The audience responded with deafening applause. This is what everyone has been waiting
for, including me, Joe thought. Gideon the
Great, the world's most skillful magician. How-
ever, when the curtains opened he saw the
water tank and a few other props, but no Gideon. Savant frowned, and Joe glanced uneasily
at Frank.

Just then a tall, lanky man in his thirties
stepped from the stage-right wing and moved
toward Savant. Curtains of long blond hair
framed his face, and he wore a simple red outfit very much like a jogging suit. Joe recognized
him and began to applaud, but stopped when
he noticed the grave expression on Gideon's
face.

Savant shared a few hushed words with his brother and then left the stage, a grim expression on his face. Gideon stepped to the microphone.

"Ladies and gentlemen," Gideon began, obviously distraught and distracted. "I apologize for my tardiness, but I'm afraid I've just received disturbing news that my life's in danger—"

A figure in a ski mask burst into the spotlight from the stage-right wing. If the figure's military-style camouflage gear weren't enough to set off alarms in Joe's head, the black tube clutched in the intruder's hands did the trick. The tube was connected to a pair of metal canisters strapped to the person's back.

"You think you're so hot, Gideon?" the intruder screamed in fury. "Try this on!"

Just as Joe figured out what the contraption was, a fountain of bright orange flame spouted out of its barrel. Joe watched in stunned horror as the stream of fire engulfed Gideon the Great.

Chapter

2

SHRIEKS OF TERROR and outrage echoed through the small theater as the young magician lurched across the stage, wrapped in a deadly coat of flames. The masked attacker, still gripping the flamethrower, howled with cruel laughter. Joe tried to run onto the stage, but his brother grabbed his arm and dragged him back.

"Let go!" Joe yelled frantically. "We've got to do something!"

"Just a minute," Frank insisted firmly, maintaining a tight grip on Joe's arm.

Gideon writhed in the cloak of fire and stumbled into a large cardboard box. The box burst into flames. The masked maniac fired another blast of liquid fire into the box, feeding the growing orange fireball. Joe was nearly blinded by the blazing inferno.

"Look!" Frank exclaimed, tugging Joe's sleeve and pointing.

A police officer ran out onstage, followed by a firefighter wearing an oxygen mask. The cop wrestled the flamethrower out of the grasp of the attacker while the firefighter doused the blaze with a fire extinguisher. When the fire was out, all that remained of Gideon the Great was smoke and ash.

Joe stared in stunned disbelief.

An eerie silence fell over the theater. The horrified audience gaped at the smoldering spot where the magician had been.

The firefighter slowly walked to the front of the stage, where the police officer was holding the masked killer. With a dramatic flourish, the firefighter yanked off his helmet and oxygen mask.

Joe's jaw dropped, and his eyes bulged out. It was Gideon.

The audience went wild and rose to its feet. Joe recovered quickly and clapped louder than anyone.

Gideon danced across the stage, bowing grandly and smiling with enormous self-satisfaction. Then he gestured to the figure in the camouflage outfit. When the mysterious intruder took off the ski mask, Joe got another shock.

The pyromaniac was an exotic-looking woman with short hair so pale it was almost white. She joined Gideon at center stage, where they both took a bow.

When the applause finally died down, Gideon said, "Thank you. Thank you very much. Now let me introduce my assistant—and the world's most adorable terrorist—Miranda Valentine."

As Gideon and Miranda set up the next trick, Joe leaned closer to his brother and asked, "How did you know that was part of the act?"

Frank grinned and pointed into the shadowy rafters high above. "You remember those workmen up there when we came for the orientation meeting yesterday? They were installing new exhaust fans. I noticed that they were turned on just before Gideon came out onstage. Since they went to the trouble to get the theater ready to handle a great deal of smoke, I knew the attack had to be part of a trick."

Joe glanced from his brother to the rafters and back. "I'll bet you think you're clever," he said.

Frank shrugged, grinning at what he recognized as a compliment. "You're welcome."

Joe stared at him sharply. "For what?"

"For not letting you run onstage and make a fool of yourself."

Joe winced. "Oh, that. Yeah, thanks. I guess that would have been even worse than pouring milk on Aunt Gertrude."

Joe noticed Miranda return to the stage in an ice blue skintight cat suit with white sequin snowflake appliqués. Gideon took her by the hand and led her to a low black marble pedestal.

"In my quest for the most astounding bits of magical knowledge," Gideon said, gesturing dramatically, "I've searched the farthest reaches of the world—from the jungles of Madagascar, the mountains of Tibet—"

"The closets of other magicians," muttered someone behind Joe, who turned to see who it was. Because Gideon's reputation was so great, everyone had gathered in the wings to watch him perform. Magicians and stagehands filled the wings behind him, so Joe had no idea who might have uttered the insult.

Frank noticed Joe's wandering attention and glanced back himself. "Wow, everyone wants to see Gideon."

"Of course," Joe said. "He's the best in the world."

". . . to the sand-swept deserts of the Middle East," Gideon continued, rushing from one side of the stage to the other, "and the region where I picked up this next illusion—far north in Scandinavia, where the midnight sun shines all day and night for half a year. The people who dwell there have changed little over the centuries, and their mystical heritage is still strong within them."

Miranda stepped up onto the black marble pedestal.

"With the help of my able assistant," Gideon said, "who herself comes from that region of the world—"

"Actually," Miranda interjected, "I'm from Chicago."

Chuckles rose from the audience and those gathered in the wings.

Joe studied Gideon's every move as the master magician positioned a folding screen of the same blue-and-white snowflake pattern as Miranda's outfit so that it completely blocked her from view.

"Now, this illusion involves summoning genuine Scandinavian ice sprites," Gideon said, as if letting the audience in on a secret. He picked up a garden hose that snaked out from the wings. "Each part of the summoning must be performed precisely, so I must insist on absolute silence."

He returned to the screen with the hose, turned it on, and aimed the stream in a high arc so that it fell behind the screen.

Miranda shrieked. "It's cold!"

Gideon snorted. "Of course it's cold. We're summoning ice sprites, not making tea."

Joe chuckled and watched as Gideon turned off the hose and then danced over to a cooler. He pulled out two trays of ice cubes, which he held up for the audience's approval. He cracked the cubes out of the first tray and heaved them over the screen.

"Ow!" Miranda shouted. "Watch it!"

Gideon began to throw the cubes from the other tray over the screen one at a time.

"Ow! Hey! Cut it out!" his assistant bellowed. "I want a raise!"

"We'll talk about that later," Gideon said. "Now, silence." He still held the last three ice cubes and began to juggle them. "Oh, ice spirits of the North," he intoned. "I summon thee to do my bidding. Shake a leg, I'm not kidding!"

As he spoke the final words of the incantation, he threw the last three ice cubes backward over his head and behind the screen. This time, Joe noted, there were no shouts or complaints.

Gideon spun around and yanked the screen out of the way. Miranda was gone, replaced by a life-size ice sculpture, accurate in every detail.

Stunned silence greeted this marvel, and a few seconds passed before the audience remembered to applaud.

Gideon put his arm around the sculpture and asked, "Now, what were you saying about a raise?"

While he was accepting the audience's laughter and applause, a pair of stagehands moved the ice sculpture and pedestal offstage. Joe wished he and Frank had gotten that assignment so he could have taken a closer look at that pedestal.

Miranda returned from the stage-right wing, wrapped in a heavy blue robe and shivering. Gideon led the applause for her. She reached down the front of the robe and pulled out an ice cube. Gideon laughed with the audience and hugged her.

"They really work well together," Joe observed.

Behind him, Dr. Savant said, "It's too bad they don't get along so well offstage."

Frank turned to the hypnotist. "What do you mean?"

"They had a whopper of a shouting match last night," Savant replied. "They kept half the hotel up past midnight."

Joe lowered his voice so only his brother could hear. "Do you think I could get Vanessa to be my assistant?"

Frank said, "Sure, right after Chet gives up food and becomes an Olympic figure skater."

"Very funny," Joe replied dryly as the spotlight shifted to the shark tank. Gideon led Miranda to an old-fashioned steamer trunk.

"Our final illusion this evening involves several dangerous elements," Gideon announced, serious for the first time since the flamethrower attack. "Miranda will attempt to escape from this sturdy tank while it's submerged in that tank of water, which you can plainly see contains one of the most feared predators of the deep."

Gideon scattered several sets of chains, manacles, and locks across the stage. The clatter of all that steel made Joe flinch. Then he was even more startled to see Gideon come running toward him.

"Come with me, please," the magician said, grabbing both Frank and Joe by the hand. He pulled them to the center of the stage.

There was a smattering of applause, and Joe distinctly heard Vanessa shout, "Yay, Joe!"

"I've never met either of you before, have I?" Gideon asked.

The Hardys shook their heads.

"Please examine the locks and chains you see before you. Verify for the good people in our audience that they are indeed genuine and quite secure."

Frank and Joe did as he asked.

"I can't believe I'm onstage with Gideon the Great," Joe murmured as they knelt and hefted the chains.

"Neither can I," Frank said, sounding more nervous than thrilled.

They checked each lock and stretched the chains between them, pulling with all of their strength.

Gideon asked, "Do you testify that these locks and chains are genuine?"

"They're the real thing, all right," Joe stated.

"I thank you for your assistance."

Frank left the stage in a hurry, Joe more reluctantly, enjoying the applause from the audience. When he and Frank resumed their positions backstage, his attention was drawn to the illusion.

Miranda had slipped out of her robe to reveal a one-piece blue bathing suit. She stepped into the upright steamer trunk, and Gideon bound her wrists and ankles with the manacles. Then he closed the trunk, latched it, and wrapped it tightly with the remaining chains. As he was snapping the locks in place, a hook and cable lowered from the theater's rafters. He attached the hook to the trunk.

Joe watched the trunk dangling at the end of the cable as it was lifted high above the stage and directly over the shark tank. Then it was lowered into the water until it was completely submerged. The shark circled restlessly.

Gideon moved a tall red screen so that it blocked the tank and its occupants from view. Then he moved to a large digital display, like that on a football stadium scoreboard. It began to count the passing seconds in large red numbers.

Gideon seemed to forget about Miranda and the shark tank, and he began performing an amazing illusion by levitating several television sets. Joe marveled at the trick, but couldn't keep his eyes off the timer. As it crept past the three-minute mark, the tension was so strong in the theater that Joe could almost feel it.

Behind him, a bald magician in a black cape said to a friend, "You may not like him personally, but you have to admit, the man knows how to build suspense."

When the timer finally reached five minutes, it stopped and issued a blaring buzz. Gideon dashed across the stage and pushed the red screen out of the way, revealing the trunk still submerged in the tank. After a dramatic signal from the magician, the trunk was raised out of the water, over the stage, and lowered to the floor.

Joe looked out at the people in the audience. They all seemed to stop breathing as they awaited the outcome of the illusion. Frank, too, was completely absorbed.

Gideon removed the chains from around the trunk and then reached for the clasp. "Ladies and gentlemen," he said, his voice rising, "as you know, it would be impossible to survive such an ordeal. Trapped underwater in a locked trunk, a vicious, hungry shark hovering overhead." He paused and smiled. "But with magic, anything is possible." He turned the key in the latch. "As you can see, Ms. Valentine is quite—"

The trunk opened, and a collective gasp rose from the audience as Miranda Valentine's deathly pale body fell out of the trunk and collapsed on the stage floor. Gideon stared at the limp form of his assistant. The magician's horrified stare told Joe this was not part of the act.

Dr. Savant rushed onstage and over to Miranda's body. Joe suddenly found himself in the middle of a small crowd of performers swarming onto the stage.

Dr. Savant's voice rose up in the confusion and blurted out the words Joe and everyone else had feared: "She's dead!"

Chapter

3

"HOW COULD SOMETHING like this happen?" Frank asked his brother. It was an hour after Gideon's illusion had ended in tragedy. "I know it was supposed to *look* like a dangerous trick—but that was all part of the illusion, right?"

"Not this time," Joe noted grimly. "And as much as I hate to say it, the way Gideon disappeared right after it happened looks pretty bad. Maybe we'll find out more from the police."

Frank glanced around at the stagehands and performers in the cluttered backstage area, all waiting for the police to question them. The other stagehands who had helped Frank and

Joe move the shark tank were there, as were the bald magician, the one dressed like a medieval wizard, Selina St. Dragon, and dozens of others. They talked in small groups, clearly upset by Miranda's death.

"The police have their hands full," Frank said. "Now that they've finished clearing out the audience, they have to question everybody involved in the show."

"It's going to be a long night," Joe replied.

"No kidding," Frank said, glancing at his watch. "I'd better call home and tell them not to wait up for us."

Frank made the call from a backstage pay phone. While he was working his way back through the milling crowd, he ran into a familiar face in a Bayport police uniform.

Con Riley, an old friend of the Hardys, was closing his notebook when he looked up and saw Frank. "What're you doing here?" Con asked.

"Waiting to be interviewed by your pals," Frank answered. "We were working as stagehands for the show," he explained as Riley followed him back to where Joe sat on a crate.

"We saw the whole thing," Joe said. "It was a pretty ugly accident."

Riley shook his head. "*Accident* is the wrong word. Try *murder.*"

Joe had known it was a possibility, but he was still stunned. "Are you sure?"

Riley flipped his notebook open. "I just got through listening to the preliminary forensics report. The victim successfully removed the manacles binding her wrists and ankles, but she couldn't get out of the trunk. The cause of death was drowning."

"She couldn't get out of the trunk?" Frank echoed. "There must have been a way to get out, a hidden escape hatch or something. I mean, it was all part of a magic act."

The police officer nodded. "She was supposed to slip out a secret panel in the back of the trunk—but someone jammed the secret panel with the blade of a penknife and then broke it off so it wouldn't be noticed. There's no way that was an accident."

"No, I guess not," Joe admitted glumly. He didn't want to believe Gideon had deliberately killed his assistant.

"Have you found Gideon yet?" Frank asked.

Riley shook his head. "We've got an all-points bulletin out on him, but no sign of him so far."

"He fools people for a living," Frank said. "If this was premeditated, he must have had an escape plan—and I'll bet it was clever."

"If that's true," Joe responded, "he'll be tough to catch."

Riley nodded. "I'm on my way back to the

station to join the manhunt. Looks like I'm not going to get much sleep tonight."

"You're not the only one," Frank said. "After what we saw here, I think a lot of people in Bayport will have a hard time sleeping."

Most of the conversations around them died down as Harry and Dr. Savant entered the backstage area with three men in suits. Frank knew the three men were detectives because he recognized one of them.

"Broussard," Joe muttered at the sight of the heavyset man with gray hair. "He's going to be real happy to see us."

"Thank you for your patience," Harry said, addressing the crowd. Frank thought he looked tired and pale. "This is a difficult time for all of us, and I know most of you would rather forget what happened tonight. But it's important that we do whatever we can to assist the police. Anything you saw could help. Lieutenant Broussard is in charge. Please give him your complete cooperation."

Broussard stepped forward. "It's late and I'm sure you all want to get out of here, so we'll make this as quick as possible."

The police took over one of the backstage dressing rooms for the investigation. The first witness called was Dr. Savant, brother of the missing magician and the first person to reach the body of the victim.

Harry paced back and forth not far from

the Hardys. Frank wished there were something he could say to help the aged magician, but he decided it would be best to leave him alone.

Frank studied Dr. Savant when he emerged from the dressing room. He seemed distraught, with his perfectly styled hair in disarray and his eyes rimmed in red.

A hush fell over the waiting performers and stagehands as Savant silently passed through them. When the hypnotist reached Harry, he broke down in anguish. Frank couldn't help overhearing.

"I feel terrible," Savant said. "I feel like I betrayed my brother. I know in my heart that he had nothing to do with this tragedy, but I had to tell the police the truth."

"The truth about what?" Harry asked him.

"Gideon and Miranda had been arguing a lot recently," Savant answered.

"That doesn't mean a thing." Harry's deep, booming showman's voice was subdued to a gentle rumble. "What were they arguing about?"

Savant threw up his hands. "The usual things. You know how it is between a magician and his assistant. She had learned so much that she wanted more money, more credit, more input into the act."

He lowered his voice, but Frank could still make out his words. "That's always been a problem with Gideon. He can't share center stage with anyone. So they argued. It was disturbing, but I thought that sooner or later Miranda would realize Gideon would never give her an equal share of the act and strike out on her own."

Harry nodded as if he'd heard the story a thousand times before.

"Gideon didn't want her to leave," Savant continued, "but if Miranda left him, he would find a new assistant and the show would go on. But the police seem convinced that Gideon killed Miranda, and nothing I said could change their minds. I don't know what to do."

Frank leaned close to his brother. "Follow me," he whispered. He cleared his throat as he stepped up to the hypnotist. "I think we might be able to help you."

Harry made the introductions and then turned to Frank. "I know your father is a private detective. Are you suggesting that Dr. Savant hire him to investigate Miranda's murder?"

Savant frowned. "I don't think I could afford to hire—"

"No," Frank cut him off gently. "That wasn't what I had in mind."

Harry raised his eyebrows. "Then how do you think you can help?"

"Well," Frank replied slowly, "Joe and I have cracked a few cases ourselves."

Savant smiled weakly. "It's very generous of

you to offer your services, but this is a very serious matter. I hardly think a couple of teen-age boys could—"

"Don't be so hasty," Joe spoke up. "You've been in the magic business long enough to know that misdirection and illusion are all you need to make an act work."

"Yes, that's true," Savant responded. "But I don't see your point."

"It's simple," Joe said. "The official police investigation will supply plenty of misdirection, and the fact that Frank and I *look* like a couple of harmless teenagers working as stagehands provides the perfect cover—the illusion."

Harry nodded. "It could work. If the real murderer is someone involved in the show, the boys could find out something the police would never uncover."

Savant stared at the Hardys with hope in his eyes. "Do you really think you could help?"

"Count on it," Joe assured the hypnotist. "You have our word."

"I'd like to think it over," Harry said. "Come by my office after you've talked to the police."

It seemed forever before the police finally got to Joe and Frank, but once they were called, the interview didn't last long.

"It's like they've already made up their minds," Joe complained as they strode away from the dressing room.

"I know you admire Gideon," Frank said, "but you've got to be prepared that he really may be the killer."

"I know," Joe replied. "But I'm keeping an open mind."

They reached the lobby and turned down the long corridor that connected the theater with the adjoining hotel and museum. Glass cases displaying advertising posters, pamphlets, and newspaper articles about magic and magicians lined the corridor, a small sample of what was contained in the Sleight of Hand's museum. Joe had always enjoyed studying the old photos of mystic men and women performing their greatest tricks, but this time he had other things on his mind.

They entered the old-fashioned hotel lobby from the side.

"This place always reminds me of when we used to come here when we were kids," Frank said.

"And Harry's stories," Joe said, nodding. "About how this place was built over a hundred years ago, and how the world's greatest performers stayed here while they were doing shows at the theater next door."

"This place should be declared a historic landmark," Frank said.

"It almost was history before Harry saved it from the wrecking ball," Joe said. "I'd hate to see it go bankrupt now."

31

It was nearly midnight, and the lobby was deserted except for the clerk behind the front desk, who eyed Frank and Joe curiously as they headed for the door marked Manager.

Inside, Harry was alone, sitting at his large antique desk. The office resembled a prop room more than a place of business, except for the desk. A mock guillotine, a vanishing cabinet, and a box for sawing a person in half were a few of the larger pieces that cluttered the room.

"You've probably already heard this from the rumor mill," Harry told the Hardys as they sat down facing him, "but this year's magic festival is very important to me. If it's not successful, I'll have to close the Sleight of Hand. The sooner this case gets resolved, the less bad publicity I'll have to counter."

Frank nodded. "We'll be glad to help."

Harry unlocked the top drawer of his desk and took out a brass key. "I don't mind telling you, I have some doubts about what you can do to solve this case, but this passkey will help you get around. If there's a door in the Sleight of Hand that it won't open, I don't know about it."

Joe accepted the key. "We'll take good care of it."

Harry nodded. "I know you will. In case you were wondering, Miranda was in room six eighteen. I understand the police have it sealed off—but they didn't say we couldn't go in. So if a couple of stagehands, perhaps, needed to go in there for some reason, I don't think that would be a problem.

"Of course," he added, "it would be best if they did it late at night, when nobody else was around."

Frank smiled. "That would be best."

The Hardys left the office and went to the brass cage of the elevator in the lobby. A hundred years ago, an operator would have run the elevator, but now it was equipped with automated controls. Frank pulled the gate closed, and Joe pressed the button for the sixth floor.

"Quite a few people are still up," Frank said, observing people talking in small groups in the hallways from the open elevator.

"They're all magicians," Joe said. "Only performers stay in the hotel during Legerdemania."

Luckily the sixth floor seemed nearly deserted. Frank glanced up and down the hall as they approached room 618. When they reached the door, crisscrossed with yellow police tape, Frank took one more quick peek around before slipping the passkey into the lock.

No one saw Frank unlock the door to the dead woman's room, and no one heard him gasp in shocked surprise when the door swung open—no one except the dark figure waiting on the other side of the door.

Chapter

4

THE LAST THING Frank expected to see in the dead woman's room was Gideon the Great. And judging from the magician's wild-eyed look, Gideon was even more startled by the Hardys' sudden appearance.

The blond magician was still wearing the simple red outfit he had worn onstage. He clutched a framed photograph in two hands.

"Take it easy," Frank said in a soothing voice as Gideon twitched like a trapped animal ready to bolt. "We just want to talk to you."

Frank cautiously slipped between the strips of police tape. Gideon didn't look like a killer, but Frank couldn't jump to conclusions. Joe followed, closing the door behind him.

Frank took quick stock of the old-fashioned hotel room: a pair of open suitcases on the bed, an antique vanity table, a dressing screen in one corner, a love seat by the curtained window, and a bureau. Open doors led to a bathroom and closet.

"I've seen you before," Gideon said doubtfully. "You were backstage during the show, weren't you?"

Frank stepped forward. "We helped you with that last trick. I'm Frank Hardy, and this is my brother, Joe."

Gideon slumped down on the edge of the bed. "I guess you'll call the police now and turn me in."

"Your brother and Harry Meaney asked us to look into what happened," Joe said. "They wanted to make sure you got a fair shake."

The magician looked up. "Don't you think I did it?"

Frank read a desperate need in the man's eyes. "We're keeping our minds open," Frank said. "*Did* you do it?"

Gideon stared at his hands. "I'm not even sure what 'it' was. It was all so horrible. We've performed that act hundreds of times. I don't know what could have gone wrong."

Frank told him about the penknife blade that trapped Miranda in the trunk.

Gideon stared at him blankly for a moment, as if he hadn't understood the words. "That's inhuman," he finally said in a voice choked with emotion.

"Can you think of anyone who would do such a thing?" Frank asked. "A rival or an enemy?"

Gideon slowly shook his head. "Miranda got along with almost anyone. Everybody liked her. Even if somebody wanted to ruin me, no one would hurt Miranda."

Joe wandered around, looking for possible clues. He really didn't think the killer would leave anything in Miranda's room, but it was worth a shot. He picked up a tissue from a box on the vanity and used it to open drawers so he wouldn't leave fingerprints.

"Why did you run away—and where have you been?" Frank asked Gideon. "You couldn't have been hiding in here when the police searched the room."

Gideon's forehead creased as he answered. "When I saw Miranda . . . lying there . . . I didn't know what to do."

He took a deep breath. "I couldn't handle it. I couldn't look at all those faces pushing onto the stage. So I slipped backstage and hid in one of the dressing rooms."

He let out a low, bitter chuckle. "I'm Gideon the Great, the best magician in the world. No stunt is too hard or too dangerous for me. I can do anything—except bring the dead back to life."

He buried his head in his hands. "I should have been the one in that chest, not Miranda." He looked up with a bitter smile. "Being the best has a very high price, you know. Other magicians resent me, and I knew they'd be quick to blame me," he continued. "This is the sort of tragedy the newspapers love to splatter all over the headlines. I could see my career crumbling, and I needed time to think. So after a while I slipped out the back door and wandered around."

"Why did you come back here?" Frank prodded.

Gideon shrugged. "I didn't know where else to go, and in some way I guess I wanted to be close to Miranda."

"How did you get in her room?" Joe asked, turning away from the mostly empty drawers.

A fleeting smile played across Gideon's lips. "I'm a magician. I can pick a lock in my sleep." The smile vanished quickly. "What happens now? Are the police looking for me?"

Frank nodded grimly. "Right now you're the prime suspect."

"You're the only suspect," Joe elaborated. "At this point, I'd guess the police are ready to lock you away forever."

Gideon lapsed into a morose silence. Frank went over the magician's story in his head as he joined Joe in searching the room. Gideon's pain seemed genuine, and his story rang true, but Frank had to remind himself that Gideon made his living making people believe all sorts of unlikely things.

Joe moved to the bed and began sifting through the clothes and costumes strewn across it. "When was the last time you checked out your equipment?" he asked the magician.

Gideon looked up. "When we arrived this morning. It's routine. Whenever we arrive at a new theater, we try out all the gear and make sure everything's in perfect shape."

"So the escape panel was working then?" Joe asked.

"Yes," Gideon confirmed. "Miranda checked it herself."

"So, who would have had access to the chest between this morning and the performance?" Frank asked from behind the folding screen.

"Anyone," Gideon replied. "With so many performers here, props are stored wherever the stage manager can find room for them. It's hard to walk through the backstage area without bumping into a few dozen props. This afternoon the trunk was right outside one of the dressing rooms. Anyone could have tampered with it."

While searching the luggage on the bed, Joe found something odd—a fist-size cube of carved ebony. He picked it up and found it was heavier than it looked.

"What's that?" Frank asked, stepping closer.

"I don't know," Joe said. He noticed tiny

seams on each face and realized that what he had first taken to be a solid cube was actually made up of a half dozen or more smaller pieces, tightly fitted together.

"It's a puzzle box," Gideon said. "I found it in an antique shop in San Francisco when we were on our last tour. Miranda loved puzzles, so I bought it for her as a gift."

The magician's eyes welled with tears, and Joe turned away.

"Do you want it?" Gideon said, wiping at his eyes.

"No, I couldn't," Joe protested.

"You should have it," Gideon said softly. "Miranda's only relatives are her parents, and they never wanted her to have anything to do with me or magic. She hadn't spoken to them in years. They'd just throw it in the trash. I know you will appreciate it."

Joe turned to Frank, who gave a tiny shrug and nodded. Joe nodded back at Gideon. "Thanks." He put the puzzle box in his jacket pocket. "May I ask you a personal question?"

"Yes. Anything if it might help."

"We heard that you and Miranda had been arguing a lot recently. What about?"

Gideon frowned. "Miranda was the best assistant I ever had. She was bright and talented. She could probably do half the tricks in the act without any help from me—and that's exactly what she wanted."

The magician sighed heavily. "She wanted a bigger role in the act. She was tired of being my assistant. But I've never shared the spotlight with anyone, and I wasn't ready to start.

"I think she was on the verge of leaving me," he continued. "I wouldn't have blamed her. I made my choice, and I would have respected hers."

"Speaking of choices," Frank said, "you need to make one about the police. I think it would be best if you turned yourself in."

Gideon flinched and stared back down at his trembling hands. "You said that you think they're already convinced of my guilt."

"Yes," Frank responded, "but that's because you fled the scene of the crime. If you go to them and explain the situation as you just did to us, they might start looking into other leads."

"It's the best thing to do," Joe urged him. "You can't hide out forever—and if the police have to hunt you down, it's not going to look good."

Gideon exhaled a shaky breath. "Okay," he said in a resigned tone. "I'll do it. But would you go with me? To help me explain?"

"We'll do that and more," Frank told him, heading for the phone on the vanity table. "We know the local police pretty well. We'll let them know we're coming."

Joe continued to reassure Gideon while Frank called police headquarters and asked the duty officer if he could speak to Chief Collig.

"The chief says to tell you he's too busy with this magician case," the gruff-voiced officer said when he returned. "Call back maybe next week."

"Why don't you tell the chief that I'm with Gideon the Great right now and that he wants to turn himself in?"

There was a choking sound on the other end of the line, and Frank smiled when he heard muffled shouting.

"This is Chief Collig," came a familiar voice. "How soon can you be here?"

A minute later Frank hung up and said, "Chief Collig himself will be waiting for us in front of the police station."

The three of them slipped back through the police barrier tape and into the hotel corridor. As Frank locked the door, a loud crash rang out from somewhere on the floor.

"Now what?" Joe muttered.

A woman shrieked, and a door down the hall to the left flew open. A dark-haired man staggered out into the hallway. He lurched and turned toward the Hardys, a glassy-eyed stare on his face and a low, keening moan on his lips. Then he fell forward and collapsed in a heap on the carpet. A dark red stain seeped through his white T-shirt where blood oozed out of the cruel gash from the fire ax embedded in his back.

Chapter
5

FRANK AND JOE RUSHED over to the body sprawled on the hallway carpet. Frank knew there wasn't much they could do. The vicious wound from the ax buried in the man's back had to be fatal. If the poor guy wasn't already dead, he would be soon.

Frank knelt down next to the body—and fell over backward when the man leapt to his feet, the ax still sticking out of his back, the long handle bobbing up and down.

"Gotcha!" the man boomed gleefully, a huge grin on his face.

Gideon stepped forward, and the man's smile vanished. "G-Gideon?" the man stammered.

"You need some new material," Gideon said, smiling wanly. "Didn't you try that same stunt last year?

"And I can't say much for your timing," he added as he brushed past the startled, speechless man.

"It was a trick," Joe muttered as he helped his brother up. "Some kind of practical joke."

"What was that all about?" Frank asked Gideon as they headed for the elevator.

"Practical jokes are an unofficial tradition at Legerdemania," Gideon explained. "And with magicians involved, the pranks can get quite elaborate and bizarre."

"Maybe the sabotaged trunk was part of a practical joke gone bad," Frank suggested as they rode down in the elevator.

"What kind of idiot would play a joke like that?" Joe responded. "Anybody could tell how it would end."

"Not if they weren't familiar with the act," Frank countered. "What if they didn't know the trunk would be underwater? What if they just thought it was a run-of-the-mill disappearing trick? Maybe somebody just wanted to embarrass Gideon by trapping Miranda in the trunk and ruining his illusion."

Gideon shook his head. "There might be a lot of people who would like to see that happen, but that routine is the highlight of the act. We've been doing it in Vegas for over a month. Most of the performers here know all about it. Besides, there's a strict, unwritten rule that one magician never messes with another magician's equipment. We take our craft very seriously. The props are sacred."

"Someone didn't think so," Frank noted grimly.

As promised, Chief Collig met them on the steps of the police station. What he had failed to mention on the phone was the horde of reporters hovering there, too, all eager for news about the murder suspect.

The Hardys and the magician found themselves mobbed by reporters with perfectly combed hair, stylish clothes, and wielding microphones like clubs. Gideon remained silent as Joe cleared a path through the mob for the besieged magician.

Chief Collig barked out a command, and a group of uniformed officers waded into the crowd and escorted Gideon and the Hardys inside, away from the prying eyes and ears of the reporters.

"Mr. Gideon," the chief began.

"It's just Gideon," the magician responded. "Actually, my real name is Simon Clark."

"Ah, right. In any case, I'm glad you've decided to come forward. We're quite eager to talk to you."

44

"I'll help in any way I can," Gideon told him.

"Excellent." The chief gestured to Lieutenant Broussard and another detective Frank recognized from the theater. "These gentlemen have some questions for you. They'll take you upstairs and get things started."

Gideon turned to the Hardys. "Thanks again for your help. I wish you the best of luck in your travels on the road of mystery." Then he stepped away, flanked by the detectives.

Chief Collig turned to the Hardys with a sour scowl. "What did he mean by that?" he demanded.

Joe braced himself for another one of the chief's stock lectures. Chief Collig always viewed the Hardys' exploits with dark suspicion. According to the chief, police work was the domain of trained professionals, not for kids playing junior detective.

"I don't want you two underfoot while my men work on this case," Collig said sternly.

Frank responded quickly before Joe could say something they'd regret. "Joe and I were working as stagehands at the theater because we're interested in magic," he explained. "That's how we happened to run into Gideon."

"We gave him a little advice about what he should do, and he gave us a few magic tips," Joe joined in. "He was just wishing us luck in our studies." A mischievous smile lit up his face, and he reached up and pulled a silky, rainbow-colored scarf from Chief Collig's ear.

The chief rolled his eyes and sighed. "I don't have time for this. Go home. It's way past your bedtime."

The Hardys turned to leave and found their friend Con Riley leaning against the wall behind them, smiling. "Terrific performance," he said, "but the chief never would have bought it if he didn't think the crime was already solved."

Frank frowned. "He really thinks Gideon did it?"

"Everyone around here does," Riley said, shrugging. "We're hoping to find his fingerprints on the knife blade."

"Why is everyone so sure he's guilty?" Joe grumbled.

"We interviewed a lot of other magicians tonight," Con said. "They agreed that Gideon is ruthless when it comes to his career. If he considered Miranda Valentine a threat to his success, he would be capable of murder, they said.

"Besides," the police officer added, "no one else had a motive."

"We'll see about that," Joe promised.

The next day Joe spent what seemed like an eternity in classes at Bayport High. He tried to concentrate, but he couldn't get his mind off the case. He almost lost the puzzle box Gideon had given him when he got caught trying to solve it during a lecture on the theory of trickle-down economics. He had never figured out the part about why the government couldn't just print more money when it was needed.

As soon as the final bell rang, Joe bolted for the parking lot and jumped in the black van that was almost a second home for the two brothers. As soon as Frank showed up, they took off for the Sleight of Hand.

"What really bothers me," Joe said while Frank drove, "is what Con Riley said about the other magicians all thinking Gideon was guilty."

"Gideon told us the others didn't like him," Frank reminded him.

"I want to know why," Joe said. "I think we need to talk to some of the other magicians."

"Will they be around?" Frank asked as he swerved around a pothole. "Tonight's show doesn't start for hours. Maybe we should wait until then."

"There will be plenty of magicians around when we get there. During the day they hold seminars and workshops in the theater and hotel—and some performers are bound to be there rehearsing or checking their props."

"Considering how little we had to do last

night, I think we could get out of our stage-hand duties pretty easily," Frank said.

"I don't want to do that unless we have to," Joe said. "Every night the show's different. Different magicians perform. I don't want to miss anything."

"Gideon and Selina St. Dragon perform every night," Frank pointed out.

"Yeah, because they're the most popular. There are so many magicians, though, that most only get to perform once or twice."

When the Hardys got to the Sleight of Hand, they checked the backstage areas first. All empty spaces were lined with props. The first person they ran into was a little man wearing a green bowler hat and a worn suit of brown tweed. He seemed to pop up out of nowhere.

"Uh, hi," Frank said, a little startled. "We're, ah, doing a school paper on magic. Would you mind answering a few questions?"

The man shook his head, slipped his hands in the pockets of his suit coat, and waited expectantly. The top of his hat barely reached Frank's chin.

"Great," Frank said, flipping open his notebook. "Were you here during the show last night?"

The little man shook his head sadly.

"Do you know Gideon the Great?" Frank asked.

The little man shook his head again.

"Can you talk?" Joe asked impatiently.

The little man smiled and shook his head.

"Then how can you answer questions?" Joe demanded.

The little man took his hand out of his pocket and lifted his bowler. Perched in his brown hair was a green plastic frog. A stream of water shot out from the frog and caught Joe in the face. The little man lowered his hat, bowed, and walked away.

"Interesting people around here," Frank observed, trying not to laugh.

"Don't mind Blarney," said a voice behind them. "He's a little wacko. Me, I'm Ace."

Frank turned to face a skinny man with a long black ponytail and a drooping mustache. He wore a black T-shirt that said Anyone Who Doesn't Like Card Tricks Should Be Decked. His sleeves were rolled up to reveal a tattoo of the ace of spades on one arm.

"Nice to meet you, Ace," Frank said, accepting the man's outstretched hand and receiving a hearty, two-handed shake. "Maybe you could help us out."

He noticed a short, plump man behind Ace holding a bunch of helium-filled balloons.

Ace spread his hands. "Try me."

"Great. What do you know about Gideon—"

"But first," Ace said, cutting him off, "you've got to help me do a card trick." A

49

deck of cards suddenly appeared in his hands, which he fanned out in front of Frank.

Frank sighed. "We really don't have time—"

"Come on," Ace cajoled. "I've seen you two hanging out in the wings. I know you like magic."

Frank gave in and took a card. He showed it to Joe. It was the two of clubs.

"Don't show it to me," Ace said, closing his eyes and turning his head to the side. "Just slip it back in the deck anywhere."

Frank stuck the card in the middle of the deck, and Ace tossed the whole deck into the air. As the fluttering cards fell, Ace threw a slim-bladed knife, pinning one of the cards to a wooden crate.

"Is this your card?" he asked, holding out the ace of spades impaled on the tip of the knife.

"Um, no," Frank said. "But that's all right. Look, we're—"

Ace looked crestfallen. "I thought I had that trick down cold." He sighed. "Well, look, it's a tradition in magic. I blew the trick; now I have to give you something."

"That's really not necessary," Frank protested.

"Yes, it is," Ace insisted. He turned to the plump little man and took the bunch of balloons. After a slight hesitation, he turned and offered them to Frank. Something dangled from the strings.

Looking closer, Frank yelled, "Hey, that's my watch!"

Ace let the balloons go. "Time flies when you're having fun!"

Frank made a wild grab at his rising watch but missed. As the balloons drifted high up into the rafters, Ace and his friend ran away laughing.

"He must have stolen it when he shook your hand," Joe said with a grin. "Interesting people around here, eh, Frank?"

A nearby ladder bolted to the wall led up to the catwalks in the rafters, so Frank was able to reach his watch without too much trouble. Along with his watch, he also discovered something else tied to the balloons. It was a playing card—the two of clubs. Frank was impressed.

The Hardys resolved to choose the next person they spoke to very carefully. They made their way through the narrow aisles created by stacks of props and the steel cage that held Selina's cranky grizzly bear. Goliath let out a low growl as they passed.

At the end of the hallway they came across a handful of magicians who abruptly stopped talking when the Hardys approached. One's face was painted in a death mask, another was rolling a double-edged razor blade along the knuckles of one hand, and a third seemed to have a twelve-inch spike stuck through his neck.

"Pass," Joe muttered. Frank nodded.

They peered into several of the dressing rooms. Most of them were empty, but Joe discovered a gorgeous young woman in one of the rooms. She was dressed in a harem outfit, and her long, fiery red hair was loosely held back by a silk scarf.

"I definitely think we should interrogate her," Joe whispered as he pushed his brother into the room.

The woman whirled around in surprise, holding a long-necked green bottle to her lips with one hand and clutching a lit torch with the other.

"Sorry to interrupt," Frank said.

The woman whipped the bottle away from her lips and swung the torch up at the same time, spewing out whatever was in her mouth. The liquid hit the torch flame and shot a hot blast of fire across the room—right at Frank!

Chapter

6

"LOOK OUT!" JOE SHOUTED as the stream of fire shot out at his brother.

Frank threw up his hands to shield his face. The flames hit his arms. Frank grimaced, waiting for a jolt of agonizing pain from the searing heat, but the fire barely tickled his forearms before flickering out.

"Are you out of your mind?" he blurted out, glaring at the woman. He twisted his singed arm around to view the damage. The skin was red and starting to sting.

Behind him, the magicians in the hallway howled with laughter. "Way to go, hot stuff!" one of them hooted as they fled down the hallway.

53

"Oh, I'm sorry," the woman in the harem outfit said with a distinct southern accent. She put the torch in a holder and hurried over to Frank. "Let me see," she said, reaching for Frank's arm. He yanked his arm away, keeping a wary eye on the woman.

"Don't move," the woman said. "I'll get you some ice." She dashed across the room to a small ice chest, pulled the scarf out of her hair, and filled it with ice from the chest.

Frank and Joe exchanged puzzled glances. Joe shrugged. One look had told him the burn on Frank's arm wasn't serious, and he was intrigued by this harem-dressed southern belle who had first tried to incinerate them and now was knocking herself out to help.

"I'm really, really sorry," she said as she brought the ice pack to Frank and handed it to him. Joe figured that she wasn't more than two or three years older than he was.

Frank took the ice pack but offered no thanks.

"Are you trying to tell us that your dragon act was an accident?" Joe asked.

"Yes," she said. "Well, no, not entirely. I mean, the fire-breathing wasn't an accident, but I didn't mean to get that close. I misjudged the distance."

"No kidding," Frank said. "Why would you even want to come close?"

The fire-breathing magician seemed to be on

the verge of tears. "I'm sorry. I just wanted to look good in front of the others. I didn't want to hurt anybody."

Frank held the ice pack against his arm and regarded her carefully. "What are you talking about?"

Joe gestured for Frank to back off. He took the woman's hand and led her over to a chair. "It's okay," he said gently, sitting on a chair next to her. "I'm sure you didn't mean to hurt anyone." He turned to his brother. "No real harm done, right, Frank?"

"Right," Frank grumbled.

Joe couldn't help grinning. Usually he was the one who flew off the handle while Frank was the cool, detached one. The switch struck him as pretty funny.

"I'm Joe Hardy," he told the woman. "And this is my brother, Frank."

"My name's Jamie Flamethrower," she said, the threat of tears fading as she returned Joe's smile.

"That figures," Frank muttered.

"Well, my real name's Jamie Hardesty. Jamie Flamethrower's my stage name."

"So, Jamie," Joe said, "what did you mean when you said you wanted to look good in front of the others?"

She looked embarrassed. "Like I said, I've never been to Legerdemania before. I've only been performing for about a year. I live in

Florida, and I've been working at a lot of theme parks down there. The only other magician I know is the Amazing Pyro. He taught me everything I know."

"He did a terrific job," Frank said with a wry smile.

"Pyro always talked about how great Legerdemania was, getting together with other magicians and all," Jamie told them. "So I saved up all year to come. Most of the other performers already know one another. But I didn't know anybody, and I'm not the kind of person who can just walk up and start a conversation with a complete stranger."

"So you felt a little left out?" Joe prompted.

Jamie nodded. "When I found out they had this crazy contest, I figured that would be a great way to fit in with the crowd."

"Would this contest involve pulling wacky pranks on unsuspecting victims, by any chance?" Frank ventured.

"No," Jamie responded. "Well, maybe sort of—but only on other magicians."

"Then why did you pick us?" Frank asked. "We're not magicians."

"Maybe she didn't know that," Joe said.

Jamie shook her head. "No, I knew you were just stagehands. But for some reason, you've been declared fair game. All the performers have been plotting tricks to play on you."

"That explains a lot," Frank said.

"I was in here practicing," Jamie continued. "I hadn't planned to do anything, but when you showed up in the doorway . . ." Her voice trailed off.

"You figured the fire-breathing stunt would make you a member of the club," Joe said.

Jamie peered down at the ground. "I guess it was a pretty stupid idea." She looked up at Frank. "I really am sorry."

"Don't worry about it," Frank told her. "Do you know *why* they're all trying to get us? Did we do something wrong?"

Jamie nodded. "Everybody knows you're trying to help Gideon."

"What's wrong with that?" Joe asked.

"Everybody knows that Gideon is guilty," Jamie retorted. "And there are a lot of people who are glad he's in jail."

Frank came closer. "Why? What do they have against Gideon?"

"He's a thief," Jamie declared. "He's gotten rich and famous by stealing other magicians' tricks. Once he sees a trick, he can figure out how to do it, and usually better."

"I find that hard to believe," Joe said.

"You want an example?" Jamie shot back. "Did you see his act last night? Where do you think he got that routine where he gets incinerated by the flamethrower?"

"Let me take a wild guess," Joe muttered.

"That was Pyro's best illusion," Jamie

snapped, her voice rising. "Gideon added the flamethrower and the melodrama, but the rest he stole from Pyro. I'm just glad Pyro's touring in Europe and wasn't here to see it. You can't copyright a magic trick, so Gideon isn't breaking any laws—at least he wasn't until he decided to murder his assistant."

"Miranda's death could have been caused by someone trying to get even with Gideon for stealing tricks," Joe said, still reluctant to accept what he'd heard about Gideon.

Jamie softened in response to Joe's falling spirits. She reached out and squeezed his hand. "My first performance is tonight," she said softly. "It'd be nice to have a friendly face in the audience."

Joe returned the smile. "I'd like to see your act."

"I think you've seen enough of it already," a familiar voice said from behind him.

Joe pulled away from Jamie's friendly grasp. He turned to face the newcomer with a chagrined smile. "Oh, hi, Vanessa."

Joe's girlfriend wasn't alone. Callie Shaw was with her, and so was Dr. Savant, dressed in his all-black stage outfit. Vanessa and Callie came into the dressing room, but Savant lingered in the hall.

"These two young ladies were looking for you," Savant explained. "I was happy to be of assistance. Now I must go prepare for to-night's show."

"Jamie, this is my girlfriend, Vanessa," Joe said. "Vanessa, this is Jamie Flamethrower. She gave us some interesting information about the case."

"What are you two doing here?" Frank asked Callie.

"We thought we'd check out the museum before tonight's performance," Callie answered.

"And we thought we'd check up on you while we were here," Vanessa added with a sly smile. "It's a good thing we did. It looks like we saved you just in the nick of time."

Joe was relieved that she seemed more amused than angry at the awkward situation.

"You can save us anytime," he said with a laugh, and then told them about the encounter with Ace and Blarney.

While Frank was describing Ace's knife-throwing card trick, Joe thought he heard a low rumbling outside in the hallway.

"Shh!" he said. "Do you hear something?"

Frank cocked his head and listened. "No, I don't hear any—"

A heavy shuffling sound drifted into the room from right outside the door. Then a deep, rumbling growl echoed.

The door flew open, ripped half off the hinges. A mountain of fur and teeth blocked the doorway. Goliath, the mammoth grizzly bear, shambled into the room, baring his huge fangs in a snarl.

"Nobody move," Frank whispered.

"Terrific plan," Joe hissed, frozen to the spot. "I was going to try a couple of kung fu moves on him, but luckily you talked me out of it."

Goliath reared up on his hind legs, his head brushing the ceiling. Then the grizzly bear let out a bloodcurdling roar.

Chapter

7

"BACK, GOLIATH! BACK!" Frank shouted as
the bear fell back to the floor and lumbered
on all fours across the room.

Frank jumped in front of the others, clapping his hands and waving his arms in the air.
Then he darted off to one side, still clapping
and yelling.

The bear turned toward him.

"Try to sneak around behind him!" Frank
shouted to his brother. "I'll keep him distracted."

"I'm not leaving without you!" Joe yelled.

Goliath twisted his head and roared at Joe.

"It's your only chance!" Frank insisted, his
loud voice drawing the bear's attention again.

Joe knew Frank was right. "Come on," he whispered, taking Vanessa's and Callie's hands.

The bear was too wily and spun around to swipe at Joe. Joe jumped back, bumping into Vanessa, who collided with Callie and Jamie. Jamie fell down with a shriek of terror.

"Hey, you big lug!" Frank bellowed, waving his arms at the bear. "Over here!"

The bear moved toward Frank, backing him into a corner. Goliath closed in on him.

Joe couldn't stand and watch the bear tear his brother to shreds. He had to do something. In desperation he wrenched Jamie's flaming torch out of its holder and charged the wall of fur and fangs.

"Hey, Godzilla!" he yelled, waving the torch in the bear's face. "Try this!"

The grizzly bear wavered, his eyes focusing on the foot-high flame as he took a vicious swipe at Joe. Joe ducked and darted from side to side as he jabbed the torch at the bear's muzzle, trying to force him back. Instead, Goliath lunged again. Joe barely made it out of his way and found his back pressed against the wall.

The grizzly bear roared once more, blasting Joe with hot, reeking breath before closing in for the kill.

"Get the others out of here!" Joe screamed at his brother. Just then a loop of coarse brown rope slipped over the grizzly's head from behind, surprising Joe almost as much as the bear.

"Down, Goliath!" a stern voice commanded.

The bear growled once, but it was a petulant, defeated sound. A tug on the rope twisted the bear around.

Selina St. Dragon, the raven-haired magician, stood just inside the doorway, clutching the other end of the rope in her hand. "Bad bear!" she scolded, shaking a finger at the monstrous animal as if he were a child caught with his hand in the cookie jar.

"I'm terribly sorry about this," she said, her angry eyes never leaving the bear. "I don't know how he got out of his cage."

"Bad bear!" she repeated, scowling. "Back to your cage, now!" She tugged on the rope, and the bear followed her out of the room.

Vanessa let out a heavy sigh of relief and ran over to give Joe a big hug.

"Oof," Joe gasped. "I'm glad Goliath didn't try that."

"We're lucky Selina showed up when she did," Callie said.

"I'm not so sure luck had anything to do with it," Frank responded. He glanced over at Joe. "I think we should have a word with Ms. St. Dragon."

After they had all caught their breath, Frank

and Joe headed out after the bear's owner, and Callie and Vanessa went to the museum.

"What are you thinking?" Joe asked when they were alone.

"I want to find out who's trying to scare us off this case," Frank said. "My guess is that whoever started this practical joke campaign against us was responsible for Miranda Valentine's death."

"You think unleashing a man-eating grizzly bear is somebody's idea of a joke?" Joe said.

Frank shook his head. "No. That must have been a deliberate attempt to get us out of the way. Since all the pranks haven't had any effect, the killer must have decided to try more drastic measures."

The Hardys neared the heavy steel cage that served as Goliath's temporary home. The bear dropped on his bed of straw and glared as the Hardys came into sight. Selina was snapping a heavy padlock into place.

"Was the cage locked before?" Frank asked.

"Of course," she said, her voice commanding. "Someone must have picked the lock."

"Any idea who?" Joe asked.

She turned to face them, her hands on her hips. Joe thought she was as beautiful up close as she had been onstage. He had to remind himself that she had been in magic for over ten years and was at least that much older than he.

"Are you kidding?" she responded. "Almost everyone here knows how to pick a lock."

"Where were you when it happened?" Joe asked. "Your timing in saving us couldn't have been better if you'd planned it."

Selina gave Joe a look of disbelief. "I didn't *plan* anything. I was rehearsing for my act in one of the dressing rooms when I heard Goliath roar. Everyone in the building must have heard him. I could tell something was upsetting him, so I came to see what was going on."

"And we're glad you did," Frank responded with a pleasant smile. "But somebody deliberately let Goliath out of his cage. Did you see anyone hanging around when you got here?"

She shook her head. "No one."

Frank studied her closely. "Do you know anybody who holds a grudge against Gideon big enough to lead to murder?"

She licked her lips and turned away from them. Then she turned back and glared. "How would I know?"

"We just thought—" Frank began.

"If you really want to know," Selina snapped, "you don't have to look any further than his own brother."

"Dr. Savant?" Joe reacted in surprise.

"If anyone's got a reason to hate Gideon, it's Savant," Selina told him. "Now, if you'll excuse me, I have to rehearse." She whirled around and stormed off.

"What do you suppose she meant by that?" Joe wondered aloud.

"I don't know," Frank said, "but Dr. Savant was in the area right before Goliath got out, and he knew where we were. He could have been the one who opened the cage door."

Joe digested the information. "I bet Harry could tell us more about Gideon's relationship with his brother," he ventured.

Frank nodded. "Let's find out."

Callie and Vanessa met the Hardys in the auditorium, and together they headed out to the lobby.

"I think it's time we devoted all our attention to cracking this case," Frank remarked.

Joe knew what his brother was trying to tell him. "It was fun working backstage and watching all the acts from the best seats in the house, but fun's fun, and business is business," he agreed.

Frank glanced at his younger brother. "That's very mature of you."

"Not really," Joe responded. "I just want to get my hands on the bozo who tried to turn us into bear chow."

Frank clapped him on the shoulder. "I'm glad to see you have your priorities straight."

When they reached the lobby, Frank was amazed to find crowds of people already gathered.

"The show doesn't start for an hour," he marveled.

"Look who's there," Joe said, pointing.

Their parents, Fenton and Laura Hardy, were studying a Legerdemania poster.

"What are you two doing here so early?" Joe asked after they had exchanged greetings.

"We heard tickets were going fast," his father said. He pointed to the large Sold Out signs in the ticket windows.

"It's a good thing we got our tickets early," Callie told Vanessa, who nodded her agreement.

"Seems like yesterday's tragedy didn't put much of a dent in business," Frank observed.

"It may have even helped," Fenton Hardy remarked. "It may sound gruesome, but you know what they say—there's no such thing as bad publicity."

Mr. Hardy turned his attention to Frank. "You and Joe are spending all your spare time here. Something tells me the other stagehands don't put in such long hours."

Frank shrugged. "I guess we're hard workers."

"Yes," Laura Hardy said. "We know that. The only question is, *what* are you working on?"

Frank shuffled his feet. "There's a lot to do," he insisted. "We're busy all the time."

"Then we won't keep you from your work,"

Fenton said. "And if you come across anything the police should know about while you're, ah, working, I'm sure you'll tell Chief Collig, right?"

"Sure, Dad," Frank said. "Don't we always?"

"Yes, you do," Fenton conceded. "Eventually."

"We're going upstairs to check out the museum," Vanessa said. "Do you want to come?"

"Not right now," Laura Hardy answered for herself and her husband. "We're happy looking around here."

"We'll meet you in the theater lobby after the show," Vanessa said to Frank and Joe.

"Okay," Joe answered. "Then you can fill me in on what I missed."

The Hardys headed to Harry's office and knocked lightly on the door before going in.

Harry looked up, a startled expression on his face. Frank saw several evenly stacked piles of money laid out on the desk in front of Harry, who acted relieved when he saw who his visitors were.

"Come on in, boys," he said, tearing a long printout from the calculator on his desk. "I was just doing a quick count of tonight's receipts."

"Business seems good," Frank said as he and Joe took seats in front of the desk.

"Indeed," Harry said. "I can't complain."

Frank watched Harry bind each stack of bills with rubber bands and pack each one in a large manila envelope with the calculator printout. Then the theater owner took the envelope to the safe in the corner—a huge block of black iron with a large dial and ornate handle. It must have been installed a hundred years earlier, Frank figured, but it looked as if it could do the job.

"Now, what can I do for you boys?" Harry asked, seating himself behind the desk once again.

"We've heard that there might be something between Savant and Gideon besides brotherly love," Frank said. "Do you know anything about that?"

"Ah, yes," Harry said with a somber nod. "There has been some bitterness between them. Not all brothers are able to work well together."

Frank caught Joe glancing at him and smiled.

"As the more flamboyant performer," Harry explained, "Gideon has always gotten more time onstage, top billing, more recognition from fans. It must have been quite frustrating for Savant.

"When Gideon was offered his first television special, it all came to a head. The producers wanted Gideon, but not Savant. They said hypnotists were unconvincing on TV. So Gideon had to make a choice between his career and his brother."

"And he chose his career," Frank ventured.

Harry nodded. "He was still willing to share the stage with his brother during live performances, but Savant felt betrayed and struck out on his own. His solo career fizzled, and eventually he rejoined Gideon."

"Ouch," Joe said.

"Yes, I imagine it was very humiliating," Harry said. "But that was a few years ago. I believe Savant has come to accept his smaller role in the act and is content with what he's created for himself.

"By the way," he added, "I'm curious—who suggested that Savant may still resent his brother?"

"Selina St. Dragon," Frank answered.

Harry frowned. "What else did she tell you?"

"Nothing much," Frank said. "She just dropped the bombshell about Savant and took off."

"How convenient," Harry murmured.

Frank focused on the magician. "What does *that* mean?"

"Selina got her start as Gideon's assistant," Harry said. "She's the first to acknowledge Gideon's influence on her career. But what nobody knows is that she was in love with Gideon. She never admitted it, of course, and

Gideon was completely oblivious to it. But I always knew. I could see it in her eyes."

"And what do you see in her eyes now?" Frank prodded.

Harry shifted in his chair. "I'm not sure."

"A little bitterness and jealousy perhaps?" Frank suggested.

Harry sighed and nodded. "But she wasn't bitter toward Gideon. She saved that for Miranda.

"I know it sounds bad," he added, "but I think Selina is almost glad Miranda's dead."

Chapter

8

"LET ME GET THIS STRAIGHT," Frank said, leaning forward in his chair. "Selina and Gideon used to work together, and she was in love with him?"

"She didn't say anything about that to us," Joe said.

Harry shrugged. "It's not something she hides—but, as I said, Selina's feelings for Gideon run fairly deep. It's probably something she'd rather not talk about."

"If she's the killer, she'd definitely want to keep her mouth shut," Frank added.

"Except to throw us off the trail and send us chasing after Savant," Joe added. "Did Selina and Gideon work together long?"

Harry stood up. "Come with me. I'll tell you what I know, and you can decide for yourselves."

The Hardys followed Harry out of the office to the stairway. Nearby, a pair of magicians in matching purple outfits got off the ancient elevator.

"Do you have time for this now, Harry?" Frank asked, glancing at his watch. "Tonight's show is going to start soon. Don't you have to be there to introduce the acts?"

Harry waved off the question. "The point of making each night's show different is not just to give all of the magicians a chance in the spotlight, but also to keep our repeat customers entertained. So I'm allowing some of the others to be master of ceremonies. I'm performing tonight myself, but it's after the intermission, so I have plenty of time."

The magician led them up one flight to a spare, elegant room with scarlet carpeting and framed posters advertising performances of great magicians, from Harry Houdini to Gideon the Great. A black sign on an easel welcomed visitors to Sleight of Hand's "Museum of Magic, the largest public collection of magical memorabilia, mementos, and memories." Frank looked around for Callie and Vanessa, but saw only a hotel employee.

Then he realized that everyone who had

come for the show would be over at the theater by now.

Harry led the Hardys through a doorway that led to a series of rooms. The entire second floor of the hotel had been remodeled to house the sprawling museum. The rooms were packed with colorful posters, exotic props, and cases filled with faded black-and-white photographs, many of them autographed. The place was a maze, but Harry led them through it without the slightest hesitation.

He finally stopped in a room where, among other things, several ornate photo albums rested on podiumlike stands. Frank noted that the cover of each bore the name of a magician. Harry led them to one bearing Gideon's name and flipped it open.

When Harry found the page he wanted, he stood back and pointed to a large photograph of Gideon and Selina, their arms around each other as they posed under the marquee of a theater. They both wore tuxedos and looked younger.

"This is from about ten years ago," Harry said. "They'd been together a year or so and had just started their first big tour. Gideon had already been building a name for himself, but that was the tour that really put him on the road to superstardom. How much credit Selina can take for that is open to debate."

Joe flipped to the next page, and the next.

The album contained more photos, newspaper clippings, and programs from various shows.

"They looked so happy," Joe remarked.

"They were, I believe," Harry said.

"So what happened?" Frank asked.

Harry rubbed at his white beard as he thought back. "Gideon didn't want to give Selina an equal share of the limelight when they performed. She, on the other hand, had developed into quite a magician and wanted to do more."

"And I'll bet they had similar problems in their personal relationship," Joe guessed.

Harry chuckled. "I'm not sure Gideon knew they had a personal relationship. He was obsessed with his career, always thinking about the next tour, the next great illusion."

"That sounds a lot like his relationship with Miranda," Frank noted.

"Some people don't learn from their mistakes," Harry remarked.

"How long ago did Selina finally leave him?" Joe asked.

"About three years ago. She put together her own act, and the rest, as they say, is history."

"What about now?" Frank asked the magician. "Since they split up, how do Gideon and Selina get along?"

Harry grimaced. "Come with me," he said cryptically, heading deeper into the museum.

He stopped at a closed door. It was painted black to match the walls, and it bore no sign. If not for Harry, Frank and Joe might not have even noticed it. Harry unlocked the door with a key from his pocket and led the Hardys inside.

Frank stared at the narrow, unfinished room by the light of a couple of bare bulbs dangling from the ceiling. Metal shelves lining the walls haphazardly held stacks of cardboard boxes. Those too big for the shelves filled the narrow aisle down the center of the long room.

Just inside the door stood a rough table made of plywood and two-by-fours. Beneath it Frank saw photo albums, picture frames, and assorted supplies. On top of the table, an empty box rested among a litter of loose photographs and letters bound in stacks with ribbon.

"This is my workroom," Harry explained. "All these boxes hold the items I haven't had a chance to go through and put on display. This is where I spend most of my time during the year."

Harry squeezed past the table and picked up an oversize portfolio leaning against the shelves. He laid it out on the table, shoving the letters and photographs aside to make room. Then he opened the portfolio, and Frank saw that it held lobby cards advertising magic shows.

Harry muttered under his breath as he flipped through them. "Just got this in last week," he said. "I only glanced at it briefly, but I'm pretty sure there's something here that will—ah!"

He stopped at a lobby card that showed Selina St. Dragon surrounded by lions, panthers, tigers, and leopards. The card announced her daily performances at a large Las Vegas hotel, highlighting the climax of her act, in which she made a cage of eight jungle cats vanish.

"Not long after Selina went off on her own," Harry said, "she got herself a very prestigious job at one of the major hotels in Vegas, mostly on the strength of her Vanishing Cats illusion, which, let me tell you, was a stunner. Impressed everyone in the biz. At least until—"

He flipped the page to reveal a card promoting Gideon's show at a rival hotel. It showed a herd of eight elephants thundering toward him as lions, leopards, and panthers fled from the rampaging behemoths. "See Gideon make a herd of raging elephants vanish in thin air!" the copy promised.

"Gideon opened his act a month after Selina," Harry said, "completely upstaging her. Selina's employer didn't want second best and canceled the rest of her run."

Harry closed the portfolio. "That," he said, "is the state of their current relationship. They compete whenever possible and never miss an opportunity to steal the show. That's why they both arrived here with grizzly bears and shark tanks—to outdo each other."

He gave them a few more examples, but his point had been made. Gideon couldn't stand seeing Selina succeed without him, and Selina couldn't stand Gideon, period.

Eventually Harry glanced at his watch and said, "I have to head over to the theater to do my act. Feel free to look around here or the rest of the museum as long as you like."

"Break a leg," Joe told him. Then he turned to his brother. "I sure hate to miss seeing Harry in action, but we might be able to learn something useful here."

Frank nodded. "Let's get to work."

Later Joe sat on the floor of the workroom, surrounded by open boxes. He had lost track of time and was having difficulty keeping his mind on the task at hand as he sorted through the memorabilia. Every photo and news clipping held a new fascination for him. He hadn't even realized that Frank had wandered out into the museum to look around until he poked his head back in the door to call Joe.

"Find something?" Joe asked.

"I found a schedule from Gideon's latest tour. It went all over the country and took almost a year and a half. Dr. Savant received much smaller billing, and Miranda wasn't even mentioned by name, although she was in the promotional photograph with Gideon and Savant."

"That's the tour that ended a month ago?" Joe responded.

"Right," Frank said, "just before they started their run in Las Vegas. Other than confirming what Gideon said, it doesn't really tell us much, though. Any luck in here?"

"No," Joe said. "There's just so much to take in."

"Well, we should get going," Frank said. "The magic show should be over soon. Callie and Vanessa will be looking for us."

Joe looked at his watch in amazement. "It's nine-thirty already? I didn't even get a chance to look around the museum," he moaned.

Frank chuckled. "I'll go get the girls, and we'll meet you back here. That'll give you a few more minutes at least."

Joe brightened. "Thanks. That'd be great."

Frank left for the theater, and Joe straightened up the clutter he had created. He left the workroom and headed eagerly out into the museum.

Joe didn't notice how deserted the exhibit was until he heard voices approaching from one of the other rooms. He knew the museum stayed open until ten during Legerdemania so that customers could visit after the show, so he figured some audience members had wandered in. When he glanced into the next room, he was surprised to spot Dr. Savant and Selina St. Dragon.

Joe desperately wanted to find out what the two were doing. He backed up silently, trying to keep out of sight as the magician and the hypnotist moved from one room to the next. He finally found himself in a room with only one way out—and from the sound of their hushed voices, Selina and Savant were about to walk in through that doorway.

Joe glanced around for a place to hide. There was a replica of a medieval iron maiden standing upright in one corner. The device resembled a metal coffin in the rough shape of a man, with narrow slits over its hinged cover.

Without wasting time thinking about what he was doing, Joe slipped inside and pulled the cover closed. He peered out through one of the slits and saw Savant and Selina walk into the room.

". . . worked well together in the past," Savant was saying. They stopped only a few feet in front of the iron maiden.

"If Gideon ends up in prison, you're going to need a new partner," Selina said. "It's something to think about."

"It's something I *have* to think about, no matter how distasteful," Savant replied. His voice began to fade as he and Selina wandered back out of the room. "Did you notice we sold out tonight?" came Savant's voice. "The public loves a scandal. If I didn't know Harry so well, I might have suspected he cooked up this whole mess just to pack the crowds in. If anyone could pull off such a bizarre scheme, it's the legendary Hocus-Pocus Harry."

Alone again, Joe considered Savant's last words. Had Frank and he allowed themselves to be misdirected away from the true culprit? Knowing Harry, he doubted it—but it was something to keep in mind. He pushed against the cover of the iron maiden, but it wouldn't budge. He tried again, giving it a firm shove. Nothing happened.

The light coming in from the narrow slits suddenly dimmed. Joe realized that somebody was standing directly in front of the metal casket, blocking his light. He held his breath and waited for the person to leave the room, but the figure never moved.

Joe crouched down to get a look at the mysterious newcomer through one of the slits in the cover. He caught a glimpse of flashing steel and instinctively turned his head. A sharp scraping sound rang out—and a gleaming sword blade slashed the air of the cramped, coffinlike box right next to his ear.

Chapter

9

"HEY!" JOE SHOUTED in alarm, rapping on the cold iron casket. "What's going on? You almost poked my eye out!"

He touched the blade that had skewered the iron maiden just inches from his head. "Ouch!" he yelped, jerking his hand back, a fresh cut on his finger. The blade was sharp as a razor.

"Okay," Joe said. "The joke's on me. Now let me out of here."

The only response was the thrust of another sword blade slashing through the middle of the iron maiden, ripping Joe's shirt and grazing his side.

Joe gasped and pushed himself down as far

as he could. This wasn't another practical joke, he realized. Somebody was trying to torture and perhaps kill him. He wouldn't last long in his metal coffin. If the killer punched a sword through all the narrow slits on the cover of the iron maiden, Joe would soon be a human pincushion.

He had seen the iron maiden trick dozens of times, and desperately wished he could make himself vanish just as magicians do. But the magicians didn't really vanish. Joe had read all about the trick in magic books. He knew there was a trapdoor at the bottom of the upright casket that led into the hollow stand below.

If there had been enough room in the cramped box, Joe would have slapped his forehead for being such an idiot. There was a way out! All he had to do was find it.

Slipping down as low as possible, Joe probed the floor for some kind of lever or catch that would open the trapdoor. Another sword blade scraped through one of the cover slits and thunked into the back of the iron maiden. The killer was taunting him—taking his time to build the suspense and terror. Joe felt the cold steel pressing against his back, and knew the next blade would skewer him.

Joe touched something that felt like a small pedal. Frantically he pounded the pedal with his foot. The floor dropped out from under him just as the blade that was meant to rip into him was thrust into the coffin.

Joe huddled in the hollow stand. It was like trying to fit into a clothes dryer. But one glance at the blade that could have sliced him in half made his cramped quarters feel like luxury accommodations. The killer would have to switch tactics if he still wanted to get Joe.

Joe wasn't going to stick around to find out what other tricks might be waiting for him. He knew there had to be a secret panel that led out of the base. It took over a minute for Joe to work himself around to find the latch.

He kicked out the escape panel, wriggled free, and jumped to his feet, ready for a fight. But he was alone. The attacker was gone. Joe dashed into the next room, but found it deserted, too. Two doors led out of that room into the labyrinth of museum display rooms. Joe picked one at random and ran off in pursuit of the killer.

Joe darted from one room to the next, each time confronted with a new choice of direction. He was fairly certain he had covered just about every room in the museum and was ready to give up when he caught a glimpse of someone moving across the next room.

Joe bolted through the doorway and lunged at—his brother. Vanessa and Callie were with him.

"Whoa!" Frank exclaimed, holding out a hand to stop Joe before they collided.

"Catching up on your jogging?" Vanessa asked.

"Trying to catch a murderer," Joe rasped, his heart and lungs still working overtime from a mix of fear and anger. "Did you pass anybody on your way up or see anybody anywhere in the museum?"

Frank shook his head. "What's going on?"

Joe took a deep breath and told them about overhearing the two performers and his surprise audition for the human shish kebab act.

Vanessa shuddered. "This is getting a little too creepy. Don't you think you should tell the police?"

"Tell them what?" Joe responded. "Chief Collig already warned us to stay off the case, and I don't know who attacked me."

"Do you think it was Selina or Savant?" his older brother asked.

"It could have been anybody," Joe answered.

"Maybe it was another practical joke," Callie suggested.

Joe shook his head. "No way. Somebody wanted me dead."

Frank nodded thoughtfully. "At least we know it wasn't Gideon."

"That's right!" Joe said. "The police are still

holding him. That means the killer has to be someone else. That's terrific!"

Vanessa rolled her eyes and groaned. "My boyfriend is thrilled that someone tried to kill him. Where do I get my taste in men?"

The next day school dragged on forever for both Frank and Joe. At lunch they mulled over the bizarre events at the Sleight of Hand and couldn't wait to get back on the case.

With an hour left before the final bell, the principal called everyone to the auditorium for an assembly. The Bayport High gymnastics team had taken first place at a regional competition, and the principal was going to present the awards.

The Hardys, along with Callie and Vanessa, joined Chet Morton. He waved but didn't say anything, and Frank grinned when he saw the wires leading from Chet's tiny earphones to the radio concealed in his hands.

"Leave it to Chet," he said.

After the presentation began, Frank leaned closer to Joe. "From what you overheard last night, do you think—"

He cut himself off as stern-faced Ms. Platt scowled down at him as she marched up the aisle.

When she looked away, Joe said, "Save it for later. It'll be worse if we have to stay after school for detention."

Frank nodded and tried to concentrate on

the presentation, but a few minutes later Chet gripped his shoulder. Joe turned to see what was going on.

"It was just on the radio," Chet whispered. "Your magician pal, Gideon, was released because the police didn't have enough evidence to charge him."

"Mr. Morton!" came a harsh whisper from the aisle. "Is that a radio?"

They all found themselves the focus of Ms. Platt's wrathful attention.

"Uh, no, Ms. Platt," Chet stammered, biting his lip. "It's, uh—my pacemaker."

"Your pacemaker!" Joe chuckled later as they filed out and headed for the parking lot.

"It was the first thing I could think of," Chet said defensively. "Now I won't get my radio back until the end of the year."

Frank unlocked the doors of their van. As they climbed in, he said, "Well, since you sacrificed your radio to help our case, the least we can do is offer you a reward. How about a pizza? My treat."

Chet cheered up instantly. "Cool."

The others laughed, but once the van got on the road, the conversation turned serious as Frank and Joe began to discuss the case. Callie and Vanessa listened with interest.

"My money is on Selina St. Dragon," Joe

said, sneaking a glance at Vanessa. "No one can carry a grudge like a woman."

Vanessa cuffed him lightly.

"See?" Joe said.

Frank frowned. "At this point, I have to agree with you. Dr. Savant has a strong reason to dislike his brother, but killing Miranda seems like a roundabout way to get revenge, unless he planned on framing Gideon."

"Magicians do think in sneaky ways," Joe remarked.

"That's true, I guess," Frank said, "which means we can't rule Harry out either. I never would have suspected him, but considering what you overheard last night, I guess we don't have a choice."

"Why do you think Selina's the killer?" Vanessa asked Joe.

"As Frank said, for Savant to kill someone else to get revenge on Gideon is a strange way to go. It's too indirect. But Selina might have been jealous of her replacement, or she might have thought Gideon would suffer more this way. She was also around when the bear was released and when I got trapped in the iron maiden."

"So was Savant," Frank pointed out. "And somebody else could have been around without our seeing them." He shook his head. "There's something else missing. There would have to be better ways to get even with Gideon or drum up publicity for the Sleight of Hand. There's got to be another reason the killer went after Miranda."

"Any ideas what that might be?" Joe asked.

"No. But maybe Gideon can tell us something."

After the promised stop for pizza, the Hardys and company went to the Sleight of Hand. The desk clerk told them that Gideon had returned an hour earlier. When they reached the sixth floor, they found it empty except for Selina St. Dragon, who was pounding on one of the doors.

"Come on, Gideon!" she shouted. "Open the door! I know you're in there!"

She started hammering on the door again before realizing she was being watched. She glanced at the Hardys, embarrassed for only a moment, and then banged on the door again.

"Maybe he went to see his brother or Harry," Joe suggested as they reached the door.

Selina shook her head. "Listen," she said.

Frank and Joe pressed closer to the door, and they could hear the sound of running water.

"He's probably taking a bath," Joe said. "He's been under a lot of stress—"

Joe stopped when he found himself standing in a growing puddle of water that was trickling

THE HARDY BOYS CASEFILES

from beneath Gideon's door. Frank quickly pulled out the passkey Harry had given them.

"I think we should check this out," he said firmly.

He knocked on the door and called out, "This is Frank Hardy, Gideon! We're coming in."

Joe was right on his heels as Frank walked into the hotel room. The room was cluttered, but there was no sign of Gideon. The water was running out from under the closed bathroom door. Hastily Joe knocked on the door before pushing it open.

Joe gasped in shock. The tap was running, and water spilled out of the overflowing sink, cascading down to the floor. Gideon the Great stared up at the curious waterfall with blank, unseeing eyes from where he lay sprawled on the floor, a plastic bag twisted over his head.

Chapter

10

DESPITE THE SHOCK of the gruesome sight, Frank and Joe jumped into action. Splashing through the water covering the bathroom floor, they rushed to check Gideon's condition. While Frank snatched up the magician's hand and felt for a pulse, Joe tore off the plastic bag.

"I've got a pulse," Frank said. "It's weak, but it's there."

"He's not breathing," Joe announced grimly, "but there's still a chance if we hurry."

Chet joined them and helped carry Gideon's limp form into the bedroom, where the floor was drier and they had room to work. Joe began the mouth-to-mouth method of artificial respiration that forced air into Gideon's lungs while Callie rushed to the phone and punched in 911. When she hung up, she said, "An ambulance and the police are on the way."

Selina St. Dragon just stood still, staring down at Gideon as Joe worked to help him breathe on his own.

"Please don't die," Frank heard her whisper.

Vanessa put her arm around Selina and led her out of the room.

"Chet," Frank said, "go hold the elevator on the main floor until the paramedics get here."

"Right," Chet said, rushing out of the room.

Callie took Gideon's hand, checking his pulse. Frank's eyes met hers.

"It's still there," she told him.

"Wait!" Joe said, signaling everyone to be quiet.

They all froze, silent. Joe had his ear inches from Gideon's mouth as he watched the magician's chest.

It rose and fell slightly on its own.

Joe sighed. "He's breathing again."

Gideon seemed to have stabilized by the time the paramedics arrived, but was still out cold. "Stay here but don't touch anything," a police officer ordered the Hardys and their friends as he followed the paramedics pushing Gideon on a gurney out of the room. "I'll be back in a minute."

Frank and Joe waited until the cop was out

of sight, and then they went back into the bathroom.

"Guys," Vanessa warned, "the officer said not to touch anything."

"We're not touching," Joe responded. "We're just looking." He paused and stared at the sink. "Hey, who turned off the water?"

"I did," Vanessa said. "It was flooding the hallway."

Something else caught Joe's eye. A piece of Sleight of Hand stationery was taped to the mirror above the sink. In the commotion of the medical emergency, nobody had noticed the note. Joe could hardly believe the words he was reading:

I'm sorry now for what I've done, but I couldn't bear to see her leave. I find life means very little to me now. I miss her too much. I hope we will be together again soon.

Gideon

Joe noticed his brother's gaze still fixed on the full sink.

"See something?" Joe asked.

"Yeah, look," Frank said. "The sink stopper isn't closed all the way, but the water's not going down. Something must be blocking the drain."

"You think we should—" Joe started to say,

but at that moment the police officer returned with the assistant manager.

"Okay, everyone," the officer said. "We're going to move to another room where you can make your statements."

After the officer left them alone in the vacant hotel room, Selina seemed to recover from her shock. She paced the room at first, and Frank heard her mutter, "How long do they expect me to wait? I have to get ready for a show."

"Ms. St. Dragon," Frank said, "do you mind if I ask you a question?"

"What was I doing banging on Gideon's door?" she guessed.

Frank nodded.

Selina kept pacing, her dark hair flowing behind her as she spoke. "I'm not sure myself. When I found out the police had released him, I just . . . I just wanted to see how he was.

"This must have been very hard on him," she continued, shaking her head sadly. "Miranda's death and the police ordeal must have been terrible. But when he wouldn't answer the door, I started to get mad. Here I was, making a nice gesture to someone who had treated me like . . ."

Her voice trailed off, and she glanced at the Hardys, who were watching her with keen interest.

"It's okay," Joe said. "We already know that you used to be Gideon's assistant."

"Okay, fine," she said. "If you'd asked me a few days ago, I'd have said Gideon deserved any bad luck that came his way. But I never would have wished this on him. We've been through a lot together. He hasn't always treated me as well as he should have, but I always knew that his career came first. I guess I just kept hoping that he'd realize what we could have together."

"The other day you told us to check out Dr. Savant," Frank said. "Do you really think he had anything to do with Miranda's death?"

She glanced away for a moment. "It was just the first thing that came to mind when you started asking questions. We traveled together for a while, the three of us, and we all had our differences.

"But we didn't kill one another then," she added with a rueful smile, "and I don't think we would now. I guess I just panicked when I realized I could be a suspect. That's the kind of media exposure that ruins careers."

"Did you get along with Miranda?" Frank asked.

"Let's just say I understood her predicament," Selina responded vaguely. "When I looked at her, I saw myself a few years earlier."

"Did you ever tell her that?" Frank prodded. "Did you ever offer her advice or suggest she leave Gideon?"

"I only spoke to her once—at a banquet for a magician who was retiring." She smiled at the memory. "We barely said hello, but I don't think she liked me very much. Who knows what Gideon had told her about me?"

"We know that a lot of people in the business don't like Gideon," Frank said. "But what about Miranda? Did anybody have a grudge against her?"

Selina shrugged. "If somebody did, nobody told me about it."

"So you don't have any idea who might have murdered her?"

Selina hesitated just enough for Frank to think she wasn't telling the truth when she said, "No."

"Are you sure?" Frank pressed. "If you know something that might help clear up this case, tell us and we'll handle it. If you're worried about the police or bad publicity, nobody has to know the information came from you."

Selina took a deep breath. "I never would have thought of this on my own, but something Savant said got me thinking. The Sleight of Hand is doing well right now. As a matter of fact, business is booming—possibly because of Miranda's death. Everyone loves intrigue."

Vanessa glanced over at Joe. "You can say that again."

"Anyway," Selina continued, "Savant made a joke that Harry might have sabotaged the shark tank illusion to pack the house and rake in the money."

"Even if you don't know Harry personally, that's ridiculous," Frank protested sharply. "If he's that clever, he could have come up with a less drastic ploy."

"That was my reaction, too," Selina admitted. "But as I said, that got me thinking. There might be more to it than that. Do you know about Harry's past with Gideon?"

"Why don't you tell us," Frank said.

"I don't know all the details myself," Selina responded, "and I never brought it up with Harry or Gideon because I didn't want to put them on the spot. But other magicians who were around at the time have told me that Gideon drove Harry into retirement."

"How did he do that?" Joe asked.

"When Gideon was just starting out, Harry was at the peak of his career. He was Gideon's idol.

"Harry took Gideon under his wing," she explained. "He used Gideon as his opening act. They toured together. Harry got Gideon jobs and taught him new tricks. And then Gideon repaid Harry's kindness by stealing Harry's best illusions. He revamped them for his own act and competed so fiercely for jobs that he drove Harry out of the business."

"I find that hard to believe," Joe argued. "Why do they get along now?"

Selina shrugged. "Business is business. Harry owns a magic theater, and Gideon brings in the crowds.

"I love Harry," she added with a sigh. "I don't know if he had anything to do with Miranda's murder, and I sure hope he didn't. But mostly I just hope this is all over soon."

The door swung open, and Lieutenant Broussard lumbered in, running a hand through his short gray hair. "Maybe I should just rent a room in the hotel," he grumbled. "That way I'll be right on top of the little crime wave that seems to have sprung up here."

Another detective and a uniformed officer followed Broussard into the room. "Okay," Broussard said. "Let's go over the whole thing from the top. Who found the body?"

Selina gave her statement first so that she could prepare for her act. As Detective Broussard turned to the Hardys, an excited young man wearing plastic gloves and a badge on his belt burst into the room. He held up a clear plastic bag containing a small object.

"We took the drain apart to see what was blocking it and found this," he informed Broussard.

"What is it?" the lieutenant asked, peering at the bag.

"It's a penknife with Gideon's initials etched on it," the young officer said.

"Hmmph," Broussard grunted. "Anything else?"

The young officer holding the bag beamed. "One of the blades is broken."

Broussard raised his eyebrows. "Really? Take it downtown and run it through forensics. If we get a match, we can wrap up this case and go home and get some rest."

Joe's heart sank. He knew what Broussard was thinking. All along he had fought against the idea that Gideon might be guilty. But if the broken knife blade that had sealed the trunk in the trick that killed her came from the knife in the plastic bag, Gideon the Great would never perform again—except from behind bars.

Chapter

11

"THAT PENKNIFE really made Broussard's day," Joe grumbled as he headed for the elevator with Frank and their friends.

Frank nodded. "He thinks the case is all wrapped up. If the penknife matches the broken blade that was used to trap Miranda in the trunk, the police will have a solid connection between Gideon and the murder. With the signed note on top of that, the trial won't last long."

Joe checked his watch. "We've got an hour or so until tonight's show," he said. "Let's run down to the hospital and see how he is."

It took a while for the Hardys to find Gideon in Bayport General Hospital, but when

100

they spotted a pair of uniformed police officers and Dr. Savant, they knew their search had ended.

The hypnotist was standing outside a closed door, talking to an officer who was jotting down notes. The other officer had his back to the Hardys, talking on a pay phone near a waiting area across the corridor. As he hung up and turned around, they realized it was their friend Con Riley.

Riley closed his notebook and greeted the Hardys in the waiting area. Callie and Vanessa sat down while Chet made a beeline for the vending machines.

"Hey, guys," Riley said to Frank and Joe. "What brings you here?"

"We came to see how Gideon's doing," Frank said.

"I heard how you found him and gave him mouth-to-mouth. You probably saved his life. Good job."

"Thanks, Con," Joe said. "So how is he?"

"Still comatose. The doctors tell us there doesn't appear to be any permanent damage, and he should come to in a day or so. He's not going to be happy when he does, though," Riley added.

Frank guessed what Riley was going to say next. "Did forensics find anything?"

The police officer nodded. "I was just on the phone with Lieutenant Broussard. There's a definite match between the penknife and the broken blade." Riley gestured to the other officer standing outside Gideon's room. "Broussard has ordered an armed guard, around the clock. As soon as Gideon recovers, he's going to jail for the murder of Miranda Valentine."

Joe shook his head, trying to keep his temper under control. "They can't do that," he said. "Can't they see Gideon's been framed?"

Riley arched his eyebrows. "Do you have any proof?"

Frank answered, knowing what Joe was thinking. "If the note on the mirror was some kind of confession, and Gideon decided to kill himself out of remorse, why bother hiding the knife in the drain?"

"And why leave the water running?" Joe added.

"Maybe he hid the knife there earlier," Riley suggested. "And maybe he turned on the water when he couldn't get the knife out again because he wanted to make sure it was found."

Frank shook his head. "Why would he care if it was found or not? He was killing himself, and he'd already confessed in his note."

"You see?" Joe said. "It doesn't make sense. And if Gideon did jam the lock on the trunk, he wouldn't hide the murder weapon in his room, and he sure wouldn't have tried to throw it down the drain. He's just not that stupid."

Joe paused for a second. "Now that I think about it, *nobody* could be that stupid."

"But you are right about why the water was turned on," Frank said. "Somebody wanted to make sure that knife was found—only it wasn't Gideon."

Riley pondered Frank's words. "That makes sense," he admitted, "but it doesn't prove anything. I'm afraid you're going to have to come up with something better than that if you want to convince Broussard. Who do you think tried to frame Gideon?"

Frank and Joe looked at each other.

"Not Selina," Joe said. "If she had knocked Gideon out and put the bag on his head, the last thing she'd want to do is draw attention to Gideon's room. She wouldn't have hung around banging on the door."

"What about Dr. Savant?" Frank asked, glancing at the hypnotist, who was still talking to the cop guarding the door to Gideon's room.

Riley shook his head. "I had a long talk with him. He'd been in his room for two hours discussing business with another performer at the time you found Gideon. One of the detectives at the hotel checked out his story. The other magician swears he was with Savant the whole time."

Frank could tell he and Joe were both thinking the same thing. The only suspect left was

Harry. Neither of them wanted to say it aloud in front of Riley, though. If the police started to investigate Harry and the press got wind of it, Harry could be ruined, even if he was completely innocent. The Hardys wanted to give their old friend the benefit of the doubt, but what Selina had said was still fresh in their minds.

"It's just too pat, Con," Frank said. "This whole suicide scenario is just too neat."

Riley shrugged. "That's the way it happens sometimes. In fact, most murder cases are pretty simple. And right now a simple case is exactly what we need."

"What do you mean?" Frank asked.

Riley sighed. "We've got a new burglary ring in town. Almost every night, somebody's house gets hit and completely cleaned out."

As the Hardys turned away from the police officer, they found Dr. Savant approaching them. "I heard about what you did for my brother," he said. "I guess you saved his life. I just wanted to say thanks."

"We're glad we could help," Frank said. "We heard he's going to be fine."

"But charged with murder," Savant said morosely. "I don't think the police are even going to investigate any further."

"Well, we are," Joe said resolutely. "We can't prove it at this point, but we're sure Gideon is innocent—and we're going to keep pushing until we find the truth."

"That's good to hear," Savant said. "I'm sure you will."

The Hardys dropped off their friends, but made plans to meet them at the mall after the show that night. Then they went back to the Sleight of Hand.

Joe felt the growing excitement backstage as the performers got ready for the show. The Hardys helped move a set onstage, where the opening act was warming up. A troupe of jugglers tossed gleaming knives and cleavers to one another, hurling bad jokes along with the spinning blades.

The Hardys watched the first few acts from the wings with several other stagehands. It dawned on Joe that there were a lot more stagehands than the show really needed. Since the performers wouldn't let anybody touch most of their props, there wasn't very much work for the extra workers. Joe realized that most of them were there for the same reason he was. They loved magic and wanted to be as close to the action as possible.

The fourth performer of the night turned out to be Jamie Flamethrower. The redhead came onstage from the opposite wing but spotted Joe and waved to him.

"I think she likes you, man," one of the

other stagehands said. He looked a little younger than Joe and wore a bandanna tied pirate style over his long brown hair.

Joe sighed. Jamie knew he had a girlfriend, he told himself. She was just being friendly.

He glanced at Frank. "They don't need us around here. Let's go over to the museum. Maybe we can find out something more about Harry and Gideon's past."

Joe closed a leather-bound photo album and stretched his shoulders. "We've been here two hours, Frank, and we have nothing to show for it."

"Take a look at this," his brother said from across the room. Joe made his way over to Frank and peered over his brother's shoulder at a newspaper article.

"The story's about the opening of the Sleight of Hand," Frank said. "Nothing we didn't already know—but look at the picture."

Joe studied the black-and-white photo of Harry and Gideon smiling and shaking hands on the front steps of the hotel.

"If Gideon drove Harry out of the magic business," Frank asked, "why do they look so friendly? Why does Harry even let him come to the Sleight of Hand?"

"Perhaps I can answer that," came a voice from behind them.

The Hardys turned to find Harry regarding them curiously.

"Sorry, Harry," Joe stammered, "but we heard some rumors about your past with Gideon. And, well . . ."

"We felt we had to check out every lead," Frank spoke up. "We don't think you did anything, but we had to make sure."

Harry nodded. "I understand. Tell me what you've heard."

Frank and Joe told him about the rumors surrounding his past connection to Gideon.

"Your source has most of the details right, but not the motives," the magician said. "Yes, Gideon revamped my best tricks and used them in his act, but it was with my blessing. Yes, I retired at that point, but it was because I wanted to, not because I was forced to."

He smiled warmly. "You see, I love magic, but I never liked being on the road, living out of a suitcase, staying in a different hotel every night. My dream had always been to open the Sleight of Hand, and it was with Gideon's help that I was able to retire from the road and make my dream a reality. Without his support, I would never have gotten this place off the ground."

"How did the rumors get started?" Joe asked.

Harry shrugged. "There's a lot of gossip in this business, and a lot of folks are always ready to assume the worst about Gideon."

"We're sorry for suspecting you, Harry," Joe said.

Harry waved the apology away. "Not at all. I'm glad somebody is still willing to give Gideon the benefit of the doubt. He's a good man at heart—just a little blinded by ambition." He turned to leave and then peeked back over his shoulder. "If you have any more questions, I'll be happy to save you hours of research here."

"Thanks, Harry," Frank said, and turned to Joe. "Should we go meet the others? I think we're finished here."

Joe nodded. "I think a pepperoni and mushroom pizza is exactly what I need."

"We had pizza earlier," Frank reminded his brother.

"Aha, but not pepperoni and mushroom," Joe answered, skillfully avoiding the basic question.

The Hardys drove over to the mall where their friend Tony Prito managed the Mr. Pizza. It was usually a lively place with lots of laughter, good times, and good food.

Not that night, though. Joe noticed a dozen people he knew from school clustered around a table. He spotted Vanessa and Callie in the middle of the group.

The Hardys shouldered through the buzzing crowd and joined their girlfriends.

"What's up?" Joe asked, and then spotted a grim-faced Biff Hooper slouched low in his chair. Tony Prito was sitting next to him, trying to cheer him up.

"Come to think of it, I didn't see Biff in school today," Joe said.

"He wasn't there," Vanessa responded. "Something terrible happened to the Hoopers last night."

"Something terrible?" Joe echoed. "What happened?"

"Biff's house was robbed," Vanessa said. "They took everything that wasn't nailed down."

Chapter

12

"BIFF, THAT'S TERRIBLE!" Joe said. He and Frank stood close to their big, muscular friend.

"It is awful," Callie agreed. "If there's anything we can do, let us know."

"What did the police say?" Joe asked.

Biff sighed. "They'll be keeping an eye out for our stuff, but they didn't seem real hopeful. One of the cops told my dad that there have been a few similar robberies recently."

Joe nodded. "We heard about it. Some kind of professional burglary operation."

"It was a real slick job, huh?" Frank said.

"Like ice. They broke in while we were out for dinner. They didn't leave fingerprints or any other clues. They took my mom's jewelry, my computer and stereo, our new TV—they even found my dad's coin collection hidden in a secret compartment under the stairs."

"Wow," Joe said. "Sounds pretty thorough."

Biff nodded. "They tore the place apart. That's why I wasn't in school today. I stayed home to help clean up. The insurance company will replace everything, but my mom's taking it pretty hard."

As the crowd around the booth gradually broke up, the Hardys tried their best to get Biff's mind off the burglary.

"You missed a great assembly at school today," Joe said, and told him how Chet had lost his radio for the year.

Chet walked in right then and looked confused as they all broke up laughing.

Biff stood, wiping his eyes. "I should be getting back home, guys. Thanks for being here for me. I really appreciate it."

They all said goodbye before Callie asked Frank, "How'd it go at the theater tonight?"

While Frank filled in his friends on their progress, Joe fished the puzzle box Gideon had given him out of his jacket pocket and began to fiddle with it, shifting a couple of the black ebony pieces and pushing and prodding others.

Suddenly the whole thing collapsed in his hands.

"Frank! Look!"

Joe poured the pieces of the puzzle box onto

the table and held up what had been concealed at the box's center—a small gold key.

Frank took the key and examined it. It felt heavy and was very ornate and old-fashioned. It certainly didn't look as if it would fit any modern lock.

"What do you suppose it opens?" Frank murmured.

"Maybe something in Miranda's room?" Joe guessed. "Her jewelry box or the trunk?"

"You could be right," Frank said, "but there's only one way to find out."

Frank looked at his brother. Joe grinned.

Callie rolled her eyes.

"Oh, go on," Vanessa said with a sigh. "You're not going to be any fun until you find out for sure."

Joe heard the sounds of murmured conversation coming from behind some of the doors on the sixth floor of the Sleight of Hand's hotel. Other than that, the hallway was quiet.

The police barrier tape no longer blocked Miranda's door, though Joe saw that strips of yellow plastic now stretched across Gideon's room.

"If I were the guy in the room on the other side of Gideon's room, I'd be worried," Joe said. "It's as if that police tape is making its way down the hall."

Frank pulled him into Miranda's room and closed the door behind them. Miranda's trunk and suitcases were still open, their contents in disarray.

"We're in luck," Frank said. "The hotel will probably be shipping off this stuff soon."

Joe held up the key. "Let's hope we get even luckier and find out what this key unlocks."

They began with the trunk. The key didn't fit the heavy hasp, and their search for hidden keyholes to unlock secret panels turned up nothing. Miranda's jewelry box was open, and the key didn't fit the lock. It obviously wasn't a suitcase key, but they checked anyway, and then rooted through the suitcases once again. They came up empty.

"It's so ornate," Joe said, studying the key. "You'd think it would go with—I don't know, an antique clock or a treasure chest or something."

Frank stared at his brother as the wheels in his head spun and clicked in place. "You're a genius!" he exclaimed.

"I am?" Joe responded, bewildered. "I mean, of course I am. I didn't think you'd ever notice. What tipped you off?"

"We're in the wrong place," Frank told him, heading for the door. "Come on."

Frank marched out of the room and back to

the elevator. Joe hated it when Frank had one of his private brainstorms.

"Since I'm the genius and all," Joe said as the elevator carried them back down to the main floor, "don't you think you should let me in on my brilliant deduction?"

"You'll see" was all Frank would say, and Joe knew he was just going to have to wait.

Frank led the way from the hotel into the theater and backstage. It was past midnight, and the theater was empty and dark. Instead of wasting time hunting for the light switch, Frank flicked on his penlight and used it to guide them through the darkness. As they wound through the narrow aisles with walls made out of stacked props, all was quiet except for the stirrings of caged animals and an occasional chittering of birds. Joe thought he heard Goliath growling softly in his sleep.

Frank threaded a path to a large storeroom packed with props, crates, and cages. On the back wall there was a large garage-type door. Just inside the door was a parked tractor-trailer, huge and still. The steady drone of a motor or compressor came from behind it, and a wide plastic tube, several feet in diameter, snaked from the rear of the trailer to the water tank Gideon had used in his act.

Frank aimed his penlight into the tank and ran its beam across the bottom. The light sparkled off the scattered gold coins and passed over the grinning skeleton in its pirate hat and eye patch. The light stopped on the small, closed treasure chest.

"What do you think?" Frank asked.

Joe peered through the glass and water. "I think you're right. I think I am a genius. It's hard to tell for sure, but the keyhole in that treasure chest looks like it's the right size."

Frank took off his shirt.

"You aren't going in there, are you?" Joe asked. "What about Jaws?"

Frank led him around the tank to the spot where the plastic tube was attached, near the top.

"There's not enough oxygen in a tank this size to keep the shark alive," Frank explained. "While you were pestering magicians for secrets the first day, I watched them hook this thing up. That semitrailer is actually one big water tank. Hear the air compressor? That's where the shark stays most of the time. A gate keeps him in there. At show time, they open the gate and drop some fresh meat in the tank. The shark smells the food and comes out to get it. After the show, they get him back into the trailer the same way."

"Maybe we should check this gate just to make sure it's closed," Joe suggested.

Frank nodded. "Believe me, I'd planned on it."

They followed the plastic tube through

stacks of crates and boxes to the rear of the trailer. Dials and readouts glowed in the darkness, displaying the temperature of the water, oxygen content, and other information. Frank spotted a red button labeled Gate. The button wasn't lit.

Shining the penlight through the tube to the spot where it entered the trailer, Frank could see a heavy steel mesh screen blocking the mouth of the tube. "Okay," he said. "The gate's in place."

"Good," Joe said as they made their way back to the tank. "I don't know how I'd explain it to Mom if you were eaten by a shark in a deserted theater."

When they reached the tank again, Frank gave the penlight to Joe and finished stripping down to his shorts.

"Did you ever notice how you never have a camera when you need one?" Joe remarked.

"Ha ha," Frank responded flatly, holding out his hand. "Give me the key."

The open top of the tank was a good ten feet off the ground, but the stacks of crates and boxes made reaching it a breeze. Frank perched on the edge and took a few deep breaths.

"Shine the light on the chest so I can see where the lock is," he told his brother.

Joe pointed the light into the tank, and Frank dropped into the water. It wasn't too cold. After the drafty theater, it actually felt good. He pushed himself down the side of the tank, focusing on the glimmering blur of light at the bottom. He got a good grip on the chest, but it seemed to be anchored solidly to the floor of the tank. His heartbeat pounded in his ears as he fumbled the key into the hole on the chest.

The key fit perfectly. Frank turned it slowly, and the lid of the chest drifted open. A glass jar floated out but caught on the lid of the chest. Frank took the jar and waved it near the side of the tank for Joe to see.

Joe waved back and jumped up and down. It was hard to tell through the blur of the water, but Frank thought his brother was acting a little frantic. Now Joe was pointing, gesturing wildly.

Frank glanced back over his shoulder and caught a glimpse of a sleek gray shadow darting into the tank. Frank twisted around—and found himself staring into the cold black eyes of the killer shark.

Chapter

13

FRANK FROZE, hanging motionless in the water as the killer shark brushed past him. Frank knew the torpedo-shaped predator was the greatest hunter that ever swam the oceans. Creatures like this one had commanded the seas while giant dinosaurs still ruled the land. Sharks had survived, almost unchanged, for over a hundred million years.

Frank would be happy to survive the next hundred seconds.

The sleek gray eating machine flashed around the tank in restless circles. If it wanted Frank, the shark could take him in a second, ripping him to pieces with its vicious, razor-sharp teeth.

Frank had no intention of waiting around for the shark to decide if it was in the mood for a late night snack. Besides, he couldn't hold his breath much longer. His lungs were ready to burst, and Frank didn't have many options.

Frank waited until the shark's circuit put the creature on the far side of the tank. Then he planted both feet on the bottom and pushed up for all he was worth.

Frank shot up and out of the water, gasping for breath as strong hands clawed at his arms and hauled him up. He felt the shark's rough sandpaper skin scrape his leg—just before the pile of crates Joe was standing on collapsed. Still clutching his brother, Joe fell over backward, yanking Frank up and over the edge of the tank. Together, they tumbled to the ground.

"Whew," Joe said as he helped his brother up. "That was close. I hope it was worth it. What did you find in the chest?"

"A sealed jar," Frank told him.

"Great. Where is it?"

"Um—it's still in the tank."

Joe stared at his brother. "You're kidding, right?"

Frank shook his head. "I had other things on my mind. It didn't seem real important at the time.

"But if the seal on the jar is airtight," he added, "it should float to the surface."

"Terrific," Joe grumbled, hefting a crate and stacking it on top of another one. He climbed the wobbly, makeshift ladder and peered into the tank. The jar was bobbing gently on the surface. Joe kept a wary eye on the shark. With one final flick of its tail fin, the shark darted back down the tube out of the tank.

"Sure, now you leave," Joe muttered as he fished the jar out of the water.

He jumped back down and handed the jar to Frank. Through the clear glass they could see a rolled-up manila envelope.

"Before we do anything else," Frank said, "let's find out how the shark got loose."

They traced their way through the stored magic gear to the rear of the semitrailer and found the gate button glowing a bright red warning.

"That button wasn't lit before," Frank said. "Somebody hit the switch." He swung the penlight in a wide arc around the gloomy storeroom. "Did you see anything while I was in the tank?"

"Nope," Joe responded. "But it's pretty dark in here, and there's stuff all over the place. It wouldn't be hard for somebody to sneak around without being seen."

"But the theater's closed for the night," he added. "Who would be here?"

Frank considered the question as he pulled his clothes back on. "Maybe someone spotted us in Miranda's room and followed us down here."

"Selina and Savant both have rooms on the same floor," Joe said.

Frank's clothes clung to his damp skin, and the drafty theater made him shiver. He hefted the jar. "I think it's time to get out of here and find out exactly what sort of treasure we've found."

Joe twisted the lid off the jar in the van on the way home, while Frank split his attention between his brother and the road.

"Feels like it might be money," Joe remarked as he pulled out the thick envelope. He opened the envelope and shook out the contents.

Frank glanced over at the pile of odd-shaped paper scraps. "News clippings?"

"Lots of them," Joe confirmed.

Frank shifted his gaze back to the road. "Looks like we've got some reading to do."

Joe checked the clock on the dashboard and groaned. "We have to get up and be ready for school in six hours."

Frank shrugged. "We could check out the clippings tomorrow, but we won't have time until after school. Can you imagine sitting through classes all day, wondering why Miranda Valentine hid these news clippings in a shark tank?"

Joe sighed. "How about a snack while we read?"

Joe debated nuking some microwave french fries, but he was afraid the shrill *beep beep beep* of the timer alarm would wake up their parents. So he opted for a bag of chips and grabbed a couple of sodas out of the refrigerator.

As Frank flipped through the pile of articles, the common theme soon became apparent. "These news stories are all about burglaries," he told his brother.

Joe checked a few of the clippings. "You're right," he confirmed. "These papers are from all over the country, from Texas to Washington to Florida—but all the articles are about home break-ins."

Frank went back to browsing headlines and reading the news stories.

After checking over a dozen articles himself, Joe finally broke the silence in the kitchen. "Every time it's the same story. No fingerprints, no clues. The burglars strike when nobody's home, and they clean the place out. They even steal stuff out of locked safes, without any sign of forced entry.

"If it weren't for the locations all over the country," he concluded, "I might think the same guy pulled all these jobs."

"You know, they sound a lot like the break-in at Biff's house," Frank noted.

Joe nodded. "I was thinking the same thing."

"Check the dates on your articles," Frank said. "See what kind of range they fall into."

Joe got the message pad from next to the kitchen phone and made notes as he swiftly checked the date on each article.

He finished before Frank and waited for his brother to catch up. Then he said, "The most recent one is from a little over a month ago. The oldest, about a year and a half."

"Mine, too," Frank said, stuffing the clippings back into the envelope. "I've got a hunch."

"Well," Joe said, "are you going to tell me?"

Frank grinned at him. "Yes—when we get back to the Sleight of Hand."

"Right now?" Joe reacted. "Do you know what time it is?"

"It's almost one A.M.," came a drowsy voice from the doorway. Fenton Hardy walked into the kitchen, rubbing sleep out of his eyes. "What are you guys doing up so late?"

"We were just reading some newspapers," Frank answered vaguely.

"Ah," Fenton said with a nod. "Catching up on current events?"

"Something like that," Joe said with a smile.

Fenton Hardy gave him a sharp look. "All right. What's going on?"

"What do you mean?" Joe responded, trying to act innocent.

Fenton grunted. "Give me a break. You look as guilty as a fox in a henhouse. The only things missing are the feathers around your mouth." He narrowed his eyes at his younger son. "Wipe those crumbs off your face and spill it."

"We think Gideon was framed for Miranda's murder," Frank spoke up.

"I should have known," Fenton said with a sigh. "If there's any chance that the police don't already have the culprit in custody, I don't want the two of you running off to try to catch the killer all by yourselves."

He turned a stern gaze on Frank. "Do you understand?"

Frank answered with a reluctant nod. "We get the message, loud and clear."

"Good," Fenton said, stifling a yawn. "I'm going to bed. Don't stay up too much longer."

"We'll hit the sack right after we clean up," Frank assured him.

Frank waited until their father's footsteps faded on the stairs and then turned to Joe. "Let's get going."

"But you just said—"

"I said we'd go to bed after we clean up.

And we will—right after we clean up a few questions at the Sleight of Hand."

They found the museum locked up tight for the night, but the passkey Harry had given them opened the door without any problem. They locked the door behind them in case anyone was following them again.

Frank led the way with his penlight. In each new room he played the light over the walls for a few seconds before moving on to the next.

"Maybe it would help if I knew what we're looking for," Joe suggested after six or seven rooms. He made a vow to himself that the next time *he* had a hunch, Frank would be the one going nuts with curiosity.

"No need," Frank said. "We're here."

He headed for a large framed photograph of Gideon, Miranda, and Dr. Savant taking their bows on a well-lit stage. A case beneath it held various other photos, programs, and reviews. On top of the case was a leather-bound binder. Frank opened the binder and started flipping the pages.

"I found this the other day," he said. "It covers Gideon's career and—aha!"

Joe peered over his brother's shoulder and saw the schedule from Gideon's last tour mounted in the binder. Dozens of cities and dates were listed, and Joe started to get the idea.

He opened the envelope and shook out the news clippings. "I'll read the cities and the dates. You check them against the schedule."

"Okay," Frank said.

"June twelfth, Bloomington, Indiana," Joe read.

"Gideon's tour was there that week."

Joe read the date and city from another article. Frank found it on the tour schedule. After ten matches in a row, they knew what they would find if they compared the rest of the news clippings to the tour schedule.

"Every time Gideon's magic show hit a town," Frank said, "burglaries hit half a dozen or more upscale homes."

"So either there's a band of wandering burglars who really love magic and follow the act around the country," Joe replied, "or somebody traveling with Gideon is a professional thief."

"And a murderer," Frank added grimly.

Chapter

14

"THE MORE WE LEARN about this case, the more complicated it gets," Joe grumbled in the van just a few hours later.

"What do you mean?" Frank asked from behind the wheel.

Joe squinted against the early morning sun. "We know that somebody connected with Gideon's tour has been pulling burglaries in every town they played. But it could have been anybody—Gideon, Dr. Savant, or even one of the truck drivers who hauled the props. The only suspect we can safely throw out is Miranda. Unless ghosts rob houses, she couldn't have been behind the break-in at Biff's place. And she wouldn't have saved those news clippings to incriminate herself."

"Exactly," Frank said. "She was gathering evidence. The question is, why? Did she plan to have the culprit arrested—or did she want to blackmail him?"

Joe sat up, intrigued by this new line of reasoning. "Either way, the thief would have a reason to silence her. That's the missing motive we've been looking for."

He slouched down in his seat. "But that doesn't narrow the field of suspects."

"At this point we don't even know who's in the field," Frank responded. "We'll have to get a list of all the people who travel with Gideon. But I'll bet it's not a very long list. A small road crew and a couple of truck drivers are all Gideon needs to move his equipment and set up the show. And since volunteers do all the stage setup for Legerdemania, Gideon didn't even need to bring a road crew here. That narrows it down to Gideon, Savant, and whoever drove the trucks.

"The killer had to have access to the trunk after it was unloaded," Frank continued, "and he had to be close enough to the backstage action to have kept a fairly close eye on us. Whoever unleashed the shark and the bear had to have a pretty good idea what we were up to. Since I haven't seen any truck drivers lurking around, and since Gideon was in jail when Biff's house was hit—"

"Wait a second," Joe interjected. "You're assuming it's only one person. Okay, I'll admit it looks like Gideon or Savant killed Miranda, but how do we know the killer isn't the mastermind of some kind of gang? The way Biff's place and those other homes were cleaned out would be a big job for one guy."

"You're right," Frank said, "I hadn't thought of that." Thinking about it now, he almost missed the turn into the high school parking lot.

"For all we know," Joe said, "Gideon and Savant could be in on it together. The gang could be hiding out in another part of town, pulling off robberies while Gideon has the perfect alibi—he's unconscious in a hospital bed, under armed guard."

Frank frowned. "Then who tried to kill Gideon, and why?" He pulled into a parking place and turned off the van.

Joe shrugged. "Maybe he really did regret killing Miranda and was going to confess. I don't know. All I'm saying is that finding that jar didn't solve the puzzle. It just added a new dimension."

"I have a plan," Frank announced at lunch after he and Joe had updated Callie, Biff, Tony, Chet, and Vanessa on their progress.

"It's going to require some legwork, though, and we need your help."

"If it will help nail whoever robbed my house," Biff spoke up, "you can count on me."

The others all volunteered without hesitation.

"Terrific," Frank said. "I'm going to divide the news articles among the seven of us. That should give us each four or five. I've also put together a list of instructions, along with my long-distance calling card number."

He passed out the articles and copies of the instructions as he talked.

"The credit card company is probably going to think my card's been stolen," he said with a wry grin, "but here's what I want you to do. Between classes, try to contact the people whose homes were robbed. The names are listed in the articles. You should be able to get their phone numbers from information."

"Then what?" Tony asked.

"Read the instructions," Frank replied. "Explain that you want to ask them some questions about the burglary. If they ask why, tell them a friend of yours was a victim of a similar crime. Most of the people you talk to will be glad to help nail whoever ripped them off. If not, thank them for their time and go on to the next one. After school we'll meet and compare notes."

Chet looked up from his stack of articles. "I don't know, Frank," he said. "This is a lot of people to call, and we only get ten minutes between classes."

"We'll probably have to stay after school or finish up at home," Frank admitted. "A lot of these people may not even be home during the day. Just do your best, and then let's meet at Mr. Pizza at four. Pizza's on me."

Chet smacked his lips. "Let me at that phone."

Joe looked up from the list of questions on the sheet, which had to do with each family's activities at the time of the burglary and whether or not they knew about Gideon's tour.

"You're onto something, aren't you, Frank?" he asked. "What do you think this is going to reveal?"

Frank smiled his enigmatic smile and said, "You'll see."

Joe was late getting to his last three classes of the day and was still only halfway through his list of calls when the final bell rang.

"I'm not much further," Vanessa told him, "and I'm tired of standing at the pay phones. Let's go to my house."

That sounded good to Joe. When they got to her house, they found Vanessa's mother having a late lunch in the kitchen, her eyes glued to the television, completely absorbed in a cartoon show.

"Professional research," she told Joe with a

wink. Andrea Bender ran a computer animation company out of the rebuilt barn behind her old farmhouse. Joe got along well with her, and they chatted for a few minutes before Vanessa dragged him upstairs.

Vanessa's bedroom, with its high-powered computer and studio-quality video equipment, never failed to impress Joe. Vanessa had her mother's talent for animation and pursued it in her spare time. More important, her computer setup also included a modem with a separate phone line, so Vanessa could log onto computer bulletin boards without tying up the only phone line. It was an easy matter to unplug the modem and connect another phone in its place. Then with Joe sitting at the computer desk and Vanessa relaxed on her bed, they began making more phone calls.

Joe tried a man in Minnesota. A woman told him her husband wasn't home, but with a little encouragement she gave Joe his work number. Through dogged determination and old-fashioned smooth talking, Joe managed to interview the victims named in four out of his five assigned articles.

When he finished, Vanessa was still busy talking. He leaned back in her desk chair and rested his feet on the edge of the wastebasket, his hands folded behind his head.

When Vanessa hung up, she looked over

and asked, "Thinking about that redhead again?"

"Of course not," he said, surprised at her mention of Jamie Flamethrower. The question literally caught him off balance. His foot slipped off the basket, and his chair wobbled wildly. Joe flailed his arms as the chair pitched over backward, sending him sprawling on the floor.

Vanessa bit her lip, barely stifling her laughter. "Are you okay?"

"Look," Joe said as he got to his feet and picked up the chair, "that girl means nothing to me. You've got to believe me."

"Of course I believe you," Vanessa said with a grin. "I just love to tease you. You're so cute when you're flustered. So what were you smiling about before you tried that double back flip?"

Joe remembered, and his smile returned. "After making all those calls, I spotted the pattern Frank was looking for."

"Speaking of Frank," Vanessa said, "we should be going if we don't want to be late for the meeting at Mr. Pizza."

When Joe and Vanessa arrived at Mr. Pizza, they found the others already gathered around a table and Tony getting ready to serve slices from two steaming pizzas.

"Come on," Callie said, waving them over. "You're just in time."

"Yeah," Frank said. "If you'd been one minute later, we were going to give your slices to Chet."

Nobody said much while they devoured the pizzas, though Joe was almost ready to burst with impatience.

Finally the platters were empty except for a few discarded crusts. Chet had cleaned up any stray toppings that fell off the pizza.

"That was terrific, Tony," Frank said. "As always. Okay, troops, I hope that made up for your sore dialing fingers."

"I'm sorry, Frank," Biff said, "but I only got through to one person. The others had moved or weren't home or wouldn't talk to me."

"Same here," Tony said.

Chet beamed. "I got two."

"Three for me," Callie said, smiling at Frank.

"Me, too," Vanessa chimed in.

Joe held up four fingers.

"Don't worry about it, Biff," Frank said. "You did fine. You all did. And if what you found out fits with my theory—" He noticed Joe's smile. "Did you figure it out, little brother?"

"After the first two calls, it was obvious," Joe said with a casual shrug. Actually, he didn't think it was all that obvious, and he was feeling pretty smug about his clever deduction.

Callie and Vanessa nodded agreement. Joe was crestfallen when he realized they had figured it out, too.

Frank gestured toward the others. "Would you like to do the honors?"

"Sure," Joe said. "We were looking for a solid connection between the burglaries and the magic show. It looks like several of us found it, but let's start simple. First, everybody I talked to not only knew about Gideon being in town, but they had also gone to at least one show."

Everybody nodded and agreed that the people they had talked to had said the same thing.

"Keep going," Frank told his brother.

"With pleasure," Joe said. "That's not all they had in common. Somebody from each of the houses that was robbed did more than just see the show. They got up onstage and took part in one of the acts."

Chet gave him a puzzled look. "You mean they did magic tricks?"

"Not exactly," Joe responded. "It was more like they had a trick played on them. Every one of them was hypnotized by Dr. Savant!"

Chapter

15

THE HARDYS LEFT their friends at Mr. Pizza and headed for the police station. They didn't have all of the details figured out yet, but they were sure Savant was involved in the burglaries—and the murder of Miranda Valentine.

"Miranda figured out what Savant was doing," Frank said. "So Savant killed her and framed his own brother."

"That's pretty cold-blooded," Joe responded.

Frank nodded. "Never underestimate the power of envy and greed."

"Do you think the police will listen?" Joe asked.

Frank held up the envelope full of news clippings. "They can't ignore us now. We have evidence."

Biff had wanted to come with them to help convince the police that Savant was involved in the burglaries, but Frank talked him out of it. Biff was too emotionally involved in the case, and Frank knew that the police would only respond to cool, rational logic. At least, that's what he thought.

Chief Collig seemed to be in a rare good mood when Frank and Joe walked into his office. The police chief actually smiled when he saw the Hardys. He stood behind his desk, which was covered with the latest newspapers.

"Good afternoon, boys," he said, waving them to sit in the leather chairs in front of his desk. "Have a seat."

"Thanks, Chief," Joe said. "Did you win the lottery or something?"

Collig chuckled and settled back in his high-backed chair. "The Legerdemania case is solved, the perpetrator is in jail, and we have an ironclad case against him." He raised one of the newspapers. "The press is commending us for wrapping up the case so quickly."

"Why?" Joe asked. "All you guys did was read a note taped to a mirror and fish a penknife out of a drain."

Frank shot him a sidelong glance, flashing a silent signal for Joe to shut up.

Chief Collig's confident smile faltered, but then he chuckled again. "I'm sorry to disappoint you. I know you were hoping there would be some big mystery that you could crack and get your name in the papers."

"I just want you to know the truth," Joe replied bluntly. "And when the truth finally comes out, you're going to look pretty silly."

Frank groaned and leaned across the desk, hoping he could salvage the situation. "Chief Collig, we—"

The police chief's good mood had vanished, replaced by his usual scowl. "The truth is that you boys have been meddling in affairs that don't concern you," he interrupted. He waved a dismissive hand toward the door. "This case is closed. I have work to do."

"But, Chief," Frank protested, "we have a theory—"

"A theory," the police chief snorted derisively.

"Just listen," Frank said, forcing himself to stay calm. "We think Miranda Valentine's death is connected to the recent string of robberies here in Bayport."

"That's your theory?" Chief Collig responded with a smirk. The hard look on his face softened, and he let out a low sigh. "Look, boys, I know you like Gideon, but liking someone doesn't change the facts."

"What if we could prove Dr. Savant was behind the burglaries *and* killed Miranda?" Frank asked.

"*Can* you prove that?" the chief demanded. "Do you have any hard evidence?"

"Well, no," Frank admitted. "That's why we came to you. Legerdemania ends tomorrow, and—"

"And it's over," the chief cut him off. "I've got what amounts to a signed confession, and I've got the murder weapon with Gideon's name etched on it. All you've got is an outlandish theory. You boys have a lot to learn about detective work."

Frank felt his face burning. It was useless to continue the argument. The chief's mind was closed, and only solid evidence would force it open.

"Fine," Frank said, rising. "Thanks for your time."

"We don't need him, anyway," Joe said as they left the police station. "We'll get the goods on Savant ourselves, and then the police will have to listen."

"Right," Frank muttered. "All we have to do now is figure out how to do that."

The Hardys went to Sleight of Hand and checked the schedules backstage.

"Savant isn't performing tonight," Joe said as he scanned the list of performers tacked to the wall. "He will be tomorrow night, though, for the big finale. Do you think he'll pull a job tonight?"

"If we're lucky," Frank answered. "Then we can catch him in the act. Chief Collig would have to pull his head out of the sand then."

"Great," Joe said. "Let's just hope it isn't too late to start tailing Savant."

Frank dialed Savant's room from the backstage house phone and hung up when the hypnotist answered.

"He's still here," Frank told Joe.

Then they took stock of the ways he might slip out of the hotel.

"There are only the elevator, the stairway next to it, and the emergency stairs at the end of the hall," Joe said. "The door to the emergency stairs is wired to an alarm. So unless he wants to let everyone in the place know he's leaving, he'll use the elevator or the other stairway."

"We can watch both of those from the lobby," Frank noted.

"But Savant knows us," Joe pointed out. "He's not going to try anything if he spots us watching him."

Frank picked up the lobby phone. "He's also met Callie and Vanessa. But he doesn't know Chet and Biff."

Within half an hour stocky Chet Morton and the larger, more muscular Biff Hooper had joined the Hardys on the sidewalk in front of the hotel. Chet was happy to help, and Biff was grateful for the chance to help nail the man who had broken into his house.

"All you have to do is hang out in the lobby," Frank told them. "We'll be in the van. If Savant takes off, come and get us."

"And then if he tries to pull another job tonight—" Joe said.

"We nail him," Biff finished, pounding his fist into his palm.

"We call the cops," Frank said firmly. "They can take it from there."

"Better make yourself comfortable," Frank told his brother as they climbed into the van. "We could be here awhile."

"I really hate this part of detective work," Joe muttered. "One of these days we're going to figure out how to crack a case without going on a stakeout."

Joe fidgeted in the van while the streetlights blinked on. After a few hours he made a food run and then settled back with his brother to wait some more.

A little after midnight, Frank called off the stakeout. "If Savant hasn't made a move yet," he said, "nothing's going to happen tonight."

"How do you know that?" Joe asked.

"Check the news clippings," Frank responded. "All of the break-ins happened in the evening, when the homeowners were out at dinner or a movie. That's part of the pattern."

Since the next day was Saturday, they decided to continue the stakeout until early in the morning. Tony Prito and Vanessa took the morning shift.

Around noon, Tony and Vanessa came out to the van.

"Savant finally came down," Vanessa reported. "He's at a farewell luncheon for the magicians in the hotel ballroom."

"There are a couple of scheduled speakers," Tony said, "then lunch, followed by an awards ceremony. Savant's not going anywhere for a few hours."

"That only leaves a few hours before tonight's performance," Frank noted. "And I doubt if he'll try anything in broad daylight anyway."

"He's staying clean until he's out of here," Joe said, his spirits sinking. "He's going to get away."

"You've still got the passkey, don't you?" Vanessa responded. "You could go up and search his room while he's at the luncheon."

Frank shook his head. "We won't find anything there. He's too smart for that."

"He must have the loot stashed somewhere," Joe said.

Frank nodded. "We could follow him after the show to see if he goes to pick up the stolen goods."

"If he doesn't," Joe said gloomily, "Gideon might spend the rest of his life in jail."

* * *

Frank and Joe asked Harry if they could work backstage that evening. He agreed even when they said they couldn't tell him why. Their friends were in the audience, ready to tail Dr. Savant after the show.

The crowd roared its appreciation as the magicians pulled out all stops for the last night of Legerdemania, but Frank found it difficult to enjoy the show. Even Joe tended to pace in the wings rather than watch the performers. Around them, magicians hugged and congratulated one another, sorry to see the shows come to an end.

When it finally came time for Savant's act, Joe watched through a small pair of binoculars.

Savant greeted the audience as he had during the other shows, but this time he didn't ask for volunteers from the audience. "I'm going to do something a little different tonight," he announced. "In tribute to the Sleight of Hand and the man who made this all possible, I shall hypnotize Hocus-Pocus Harry himself!"

The crowd had applauded Harry's every appearance as emcee, and they clapped even harder now. Harry walked out of the wings, beaming at the crowd, and joined the hypnotist at center stage.

He leaned toward the microphone and said, "If you make me do Elvis, you're not coming back next year."

The audience laughed, and Savant smiled.

"No, no," the hypnotist assured him. "I promise, you'll leave this stage with your dignity intact."

Savant instructed Harry to sit down in one of a pair of chairs and did the same trick he had performed on Biff's father. He made Harry as stiff as a plank and laid him across the back of the two chairs.

"Savant is whispering something to Harry," Joe said, watching the act through the binoculars. "When his back is to the audience, he's saying something in Harry's ear."

Frank squinted at the stage, wishing he could get a closer view of the action.

"Harry's lips are moving," Joe reported as Savant leaned over the entranced magician to replace one chair with a gleaming sword.

Frank caught the subtle movement of Harry's lips. He never would have noticed if he wasn't looking for it.

Joe kept a sharp watch on every move of the act, but he didn't catch anything else that seemed out of place.

After Savant snapped his fingers and Harry blinked back into awareness, the audience showered them both with applause. Together, the hypnotist and the magician bowed and thanked the audience.

"And now," Savant announced, "I am honored to introduce one of the world's greatest illusionists—Selina St. Dragon!"

As the curtain parted to reveal Selina and her caged bear, a cloud of colored smoke erupted and engulfed Savant. When the smoke cleared, the hypnotist was gone.

"He never did that before!" Frank exclaimed. "He's making a break for it, and Biff and the others are still in the audience! Our plans are shot!"

Joe grabbed his brother's arm. "I think I know where he's going."

Frank stared at his brother. "Where?"

"Follow me." Joe sprinted for the backstage exit.

"Where are we going?" Frank demanded.

"You'll see," Joe told him.

Joe pushed through the heavy fire door and into the parking lot behind the theater. He ran toward the hotel.

"Come on, Joe," Frank called out as they dodged between parked cars. "Give me a hint."

Joe reached the back door of the hotel. "It'll come to you," he said. Between the rush of excitement and his brother's rare state of confusion, he was having a great time.

The passkey got them into the vacant laundry room, and from there they found their way to the back hallway on the first floor. The door to Harry's office was closed.

"The safe!" Frank said, finally getting it.

"Very good," Joe told him. "Now let's see if we're right."

The Hardys burst into the office. Savant whirled around from the open safe, dropping a bag stuffed with cash.

"It's all over, Savant," Joe said.

The hypnotist didn't seem too surprised to see them. "How true," he said with a thin smile. "Did you know that hypnotism is not my only skill?"

He showed them his empty hands, back and front, and then brought them together. When he pulled them apart again, his left hand held a tiny derringer.

"It only holds two shots," the hypnotist said, "but that appears to be all I'll need."

Chapter

16

SAVANT AIMED the double-barreled gun at the Hardys. The derringer was small, but Frank knew it packed a big enough punch to kill.

"Close the door," Savant commanded. "If you try to run, I'll be forced to shoot."

"Like you're not going to, anyway," Joe muttered.

Frank turned to follow Savant's order. He knew that closing the door would seal their doom. With no witnesses and the solid oak door to muffle the shots, there would be nothing to stop Savant from killing them.

Frank's hand moved slowly toward the doorknob—but then flashed to the light switch on the wall. He punched the switch, plunging the office into darkness, and dove out of the line of fire. A shot rang out as Frank hit the floor. He scrambled to his feet and lunged at the hypnotist.

Savant jumped aside, but Frank managed to grab a fistful of his shirt. Savant slammed his elbow into Frank's eye, sending Frank reeling backward to stumble over something and crash into the wall.

The lights winked back on, and Savant stood by the switch with the derringer pointed at Frank. Joe was nowhere in sight. Savant glanced into the hallway and then closed the door. He yanked open the curtain of the vanishing cabinet next to the door, but it was empty.

"Well, your brother and I have something in common," Savant said. "He doesn't care what happens to his own brother. He's only looking out for number one." The hypnotist chuckled bitterly. "Brotherhood is so overrated."

Joe would bring help, Frank told himself. In the meantime he had to stall Savant for as long as possible.

"We have our differences," Frank said, "but we never tried to kill each other—or frame the other for murder."

Savant shrugged. "You're still young." He waved the gun toward the safe. "Now, pick up that bag and get the rest of the money."

"Tell me something," Frank said as he

picked up the sack. "Did you plan to frame Gideon for Miranda's death from the beginning, or did you throw that in later?"

Savant smiled. "I kept my options open. I stole his penknife and used it to jam the escape panel. Then I hid the knife in a safe place, in case I might need it again.

"You and your brother turned out to be quite an unwelcome surprise," he continued. "When you started to get too close, I planted the knife in Gideon's room. I thought that bit of evidence would be enough to convince anybody—including you."

"Why did you allow us to investigate in the first place?" Frank demanded. He was taking his time cleaning the money out of the safe, dropping one envelope at a time into the bag.

"I didn't really expect you to find out anything," Savant said. "And to make sure you didn't, I passed the word to the other performers to give you a hard time."

"But the other magicians only played practical jokes on us," Frank said. "You were the one behind the really dangerous stuff, weren't you? You tried to scare us off with the bear. When that didn't work, you tried to stab Joe in the iron maiden. And it was you who sent the shark after me."

Savant sighed. "The two of you proved more difficult to kill than I would have guessed."

"So did Gideon," Frank responded. He

dropped the last packet of cash into the sack and turned toward Savant, holding out the bag. "You'd already framed him for Miranda's murder. Why did you try to kill him?"

"Miranda had discovered my little secret," Savant said, scowling at the memory. "She tried to blackmail me to get money so she could leave Gideon and start her own act. I didn't know if she had told Gideon anything, but he was starting to suspect."

"So you've been committing the burglaries all by yourself?" Frank asked.

Savant looked impressed. "Very good, detective," he said. "Tell me, how much more have you figured out?"

"You'd pick people out of the audience for your act—"

"Not just any people," Savant corrected. "People who dressed well, people who looked like they would have nice big homes full of expensive things."

"Then you'd hypnotize them onstage and find out where they lived, just like you found out the combination to Harry's safe. You'd whisper commands to them. If anybody in the audience noticed, they would think you were just reinforcing the trance. You were the only one close enough to hear the subject's reply." An idea suddenly struck Frank. "While they were in the trance, they'd tell you anything you wanted to know, including where they hid the really valuable stuff."

"Very good, but you've missed the most important part," Savant said, clearly unable to resist showing off. "I implanted a posthypnotic suggestion. For instance, I might tell a man that tomorrow night at six o'clock he will feel like taking his whole family out to dinner."

"Then you'd just wait until six, knowing you'd have the place to yourself for an hour or two."

"Ah, it was a sweet setup," Savant bragged. "I'm sorry to see it end. Of course, I'd still be able to pursue my lucrative secret career if not for you and your brother."

"Us?" Frank said. "If you hadn't decided to rob Harry, you'd have gotten away clean."

Savant shook his head. "Didn't you hear? Gideon regained consciousness this morning. He's still foggy about how he ended up trying to breathe through a plastic bag, but eventually he'll remember I was in his room right before he got knocked over the head. Then he'll tell the police."

He studied Frank with cold eyes. "This mess is all your fault. I'm not going to feel at all bad about killing you. Put the bag on the desk."

Savant cocked the derringer with his thumb. Frank glimpsed a faint flutter from the curtain on the vanishing cabinet. He shifted his gaze back to the gun. He didn't want to draw Savant's attention to the magic prop behind him.

"One more question," Frank said as he plopped the sack of money on the desk. "How did you get that other performer to lie for you and give you an alibi? He swore you'd been together for two solid hours, but you actually slipped out to stage your brother's suicide."

Savant sneered. "I'm surprised at you. That one's obvious. I hypnotized him. As far as he knows, we really were together for two solid hours."

Frank smiled as a hand whipped aside the curtain of the vanishing cabinet. "I guess you're just too clever for us."

Joe leaped out and grabbed Savant from behind, clutching the hypnotist's wrist and wrenching his gun hand down and to the side. The pistol went off with a sharp *pop,* and the last bullet plowed into the floor.

Joe jerked the man around roughly and slammed a solid right into Savant's jaw. The hypnotist crumpled to the floor.

"Nice job," Frank said, gesturing to the vanishing cabinet. "Savant checked inside there. How did you pull that trick off?"

"It wasn't a trick," Joe corrected. "It was an illusion."

Frank rolled his eyes. "Okay. What's the secret of that illusion?"

Joe smiled and winked. "A good magician never reveals his secrets."

The next afternoon found Frank and Joe once again at the Sleight of Hand. Legerdemania was over, and volunteers were helping the magicians pack up their gear.

Callie, Vanessa, and Chet showed up and helped the Hardys sweep the stage floor. They were just finishing when Harry came in from the lobby, beaming with a smile that lit up his whole face.

"I just met with my accountant," he announced, his voice booming through the theater. Everybody looked up and others emerged from the wings to listen. "Because of the resounding success of Legerdemania this year, the Sleight of Hand will remain open for the foreseeable future."

Frank and Joe cheered with the others, and victory whoops reverberated from backstage as the news spread.

"I owe you special thanks," the magician said to Frank and Joe. "Legerdemania's success wouldn't have mattered if Savant had made off with the box office receipts."

"All part of our volunteer services," Joe replied.

Frank dug the passkey out of his pocket and returned it to Harry. "I don't think we'll be needing this anymore."

The lobby doors swept open again, and Selina St. Dragon walked in on the arm of Gideon the Great. Selina kept a concerned eye on him as they made their way down the aisle. Gideon walked a little shakily but otherwise seemed all right.

"Look who's on the loose," Harry said, giving Gideon a paternal hug.

Gideon nodded to the Hardys. "I want to thank you for all your help. If it weren't for you, I'd be in jail now—or in a coffin."

"Our pleasure," Frank told him.

"Harry," Joe urged, "tell them the good news."

Harry told Gideon and Selina that he would be able to keep the Sleight of Hand open, and the other two magicians congratulated him. Then Selina smiled at Gideon, and Frank could tell that something was going on between them.

"We have some news of our own," Selina said. "We're getting our acts together, so to speak. We're going to perform together on equal terms."

Everyone congratulated them at once.

Gideon accepted it all with a smile and said, "Everything that's happened over the past few days has really made me think. I realized the happiest time of my life was when I was with Selina."

"And I figured I might as well share my secrets with him," Selina added with a good-natured jab at Gideon's ribs. "At least that way he can't steal them."